Sarah felt something hot and dark deep in her stomach. The letter had come just that morning from Wellesley College. The early decision welcomed Marla to the class of 1965. Marla had wanted to go straightaway to Juilliard, but her parents had insisted that she not start off in a music school. After two years in a liberal arts school she could transfer. There was a wonderful pianist in Boston with whom she would study while she was at Wellesley. It was all settled now. This time next year, Sarah thought, Marla would be in college, the men and women of the New Frontier on the march. Where would she, Sarah Eloise Benjamin, be, she wondered. Not on the New Frontier. Nope, she'd be sleeping to stage right just outside of Bethlehem, looking toward a tinfoil star into a conditional future.

## QUANTITY SALES

# Kathryn Lasky

# PAGEANT

LAUREL-LEAF BOOKS

LAUREL-LEAF BOOKS bring together under a single imprint outstanding
works of fiction and nonfiction particularly suitable for young adult readers,
both in and out of the classroom. Charles F. Reasoner, Professor Emeritus of
Children's Literature and Reading, New York University, is consultant to this
series.

Published by
Dell Publishing
a division of
The Bantam Doubleday Dell Publishing Group, Inc.
666 Fifth Avenue
New York, New York 10103

ISBN: 0-440-20161-6

RL: 6.6

Reprinted by arrangement with Macmillan Publishing Company

Printed in the United States of America

September 1988

10 9 8 7 6 5 4 3 2 1

KRI

# PAGEANT

# PART I

## NOVEMBER 1960

# Chapter One

" 'There was in the days of Herod, the king of Judea, a certain priest named Zacharias. . . .' "

The crisp voice rang out in the darkened auditorium. Onstage a single spot glowed, softly illuminating the outline of a tinfoil star that was suspended by fishing line.

Sarah Benjamin lay in a heap to stage right with three other shepherds.

"Did you ever notice"—Sarah could feel the warm, soft whisper right in her ear—"how Miss Crowninshield's Scottish accent increases when she narrates the Christmas pageant?"

"You're spitting in my ear, Bauer," Sarah replied.

"Sorry, but did you notice?"

"Yeah. How long has this rehearsal been going on?"

"Too long!" muttered a third shepherd's voice at Sarah's feet.

"What time is it?" Elaine Bauer asked.

"Who knows?" said another shepherd. "And, Sarah Benjamin, would you kindly get your head out of my gut!"

"Sorry. You talking clock time or pageant time?" Sarah whispered.

"Both."

Sarah paused and listened to Miss Crowninshield.

" 'And in the sixth month the angel Gabriel was sent from God unto a city of Galilee. . . .' "

"Well," resumed Sarah, "we are approaching the big moment, guys."

"The way we all hope it won't happen to us," giggled Phoebe Buxton, the shepherd whose gut Sarah's head was poking.

"The big I.C."

"I.C.?" asked Hillary Daniels, the shepherd at Sarah's feet.

"Immaculate Conception," Elaine said. "So what time is it clock-wise? And, Buxton, when we get up to go look at the baby Jesus, kindly do not crack me on the head with your shepherd's crook as you have in every rehearsal so far."

"Let's see," said Sarah. "What time? Let me turn my luminescent dial toward the star of Bethlehem. Ten forty-five."

"That does sound kind of sacrilegious—almost un-Christian."

"I'm not Christian," Sarah whispered. "And it's not sacrilegious." She paused. *"I Was a Teenage Jewish Shepherd from Suburban Indianapolis."* She giggled.

"Do you really think they slept this way?" Phoebe whispered.

"Who? Shepherds?" Sarah asked.

"Yeah," said Phoebe, "in days of yore."

"God only knows," Elaine whispered.

"He probably does," said Sarah softly.

"Benjamin," hissed Phoebe, "you really lack any kind of awe for this."

"Look, Buxton," Sarah replied. "We've been heaped in this pile for fifty-five minutes. We have not 'volunteered' to be shepherds; we have been drafted. We are not blonde enough to be angels, and our voices aren't good enough for the three kings or Mary. They're not even good enough for the all-school chorus. Needless to say, this does not inspire religious awe in me—being a shepherd by default. It's the lowest you can be in this pageant. We are the trilobites of this pageant. Don't kid yourself."

"It's a stage part, at least," whispered Hillary. "I was in the chorus last year. This is slightly more interesting, and we don't have to stand for two hours."

" 'Fear not, Mary: for thou hast found favor with God.' " The Scottish lilt washed over the dimmed footlights.

"Some favor!" Sarah muttered.

" 'And, behold,' " the voice continued, " 'thou shalt conceive in thy womb, and bring forth a son.' "

"Do you think we'll all die virgins?" Hillary whispered.

"If Buxton cracks you on the head with her crook and you suffer a cerebral hemorrhage in the next five minutes—yes. You will die a virgin," Sarah intoned. They all giggled at this and their cheesecloth robes shook with their laughter.

"Shepherds!" barked the voice. "Lights please! Stage manager, turn on the lights!" A small, compact woman with hair the color of pewter and a tartan-plaid, double-breasted suit marched up to the stage from her seat in the front row where she had sat reading the Gospel of St. Luke by flashlight. Her orthopedic oxfords thwacked on the auditorium floor.

The heap of cheesecloth robes and tunics squirmed as the four shepherds disentangled themselves from their "slumber" and sat at attention, somber under their head drapery as they awaited Crowninshield's wrath.

"I've had enough of this kind of behavior!" she snapped. Then she stopped abruptly. Her pale eyes fastened on Sarah's head. "Sarah Benjamin, just what is that affixed to your burnoose?"

"To my what?" Sarah asked in a small voice.

"Your burnoose—the hooded cape. What is that on the headband?"

"Oh! It's my Kennedy for President pin," said Sarah energetically.

"So I see." The colorless eyes narrowed, beaming disapproval.

Sarah's mind raced. What violation had she committed? All fall everyone had been wearing candidate pins. Granted, 99 and

4

44/100 percent of the student body wore Nixon and Lodge pins. The school, Stuart Hall, like the rest of Indianapolis, was heavily Republican; but a handful of students like herself, her sister Marla (a senior), and her own best friend, Elaine Bauer, were Democrats and ardent Kennedy fans. She looked out the corner of her eye to where Marla sat at the piano. Marla, a musical prodigy, was the pianist for the pageant. She was wearing her Kennedy pin—two pins, as a matter of fact—right on her school uniform. Had Sarah somehow transgressed by actually wearing hers onstage? Was this some sort of church-and-state thing? No, that was too subtle for Crowninshield. Besides, Stuart Hall was continually mixing up church and state. It was not supposed to be a religious school, but here she, with all the other students, was spending eight to ten hours a week rehearsing a Christmas pageant. Was this a constitutional issue? Why the heck could she wear her darned Kennedy pin on her uniform but not on a burnoose?

"This is totally inappropriate, Sarah, that you should be wearing an election button in the school Christmas pageant. Mr. Kennedy's visage, although considered handsome by some, constitutes a distraction onstage and has no business in the pageant. We are concerned here with the nativity as presented in the Gospel of St. Luke. The central characters are Christ our Lord, Mary, Joseph, the three kings, the three angels, assorted shepherds, and *not* Mr. Kennedy, regardless of his political views. Do you understand?"

"Yes." No, she did not understand at all.

"Now for the rest of you shepherds." The diatribe shifted and Crowninshield addressed the "issue of incessant whispering and rowdyism" among the shepherds.

"Did you believe that scene? I mean, I ask you!" Sarah said, sliding into her seat next to Lisa Cody in French.

5

"I think we should all wear our election pins onstage next time," Elaine said. "Would you wear one, Lynn?" She turned to a lovely girl with white-blonde hair that fell straight to her shoulders.

"Oh, I don't know. If Miss Crowninshield was upset about shepherds wearing pins, can you imagine how she would feel about the angels?"

"Well, at least you're for Nixon," Elaine said.

"Yeah," said Sarah. "A Republican angel wouldn't be that disturbing to her, I'm sure."

*"Qu'est-ce qu'il y a, mes chéries? Qu'y a-t-il?"* A sixtyish woman with a lather of gray curls piled on top of her head bustled into the room. Artfully arranged around her shoulders was a shawl of deep pink secured in front by an elaborate brooch. At the neck of her blouse was a paisley scarf tied into a floppy bow that hung just so. Bracelets dangled, a tasseled belt swished. Her ringed fingers clutched a piece of chalk. As she wrote the daily vocabulary on the board she chattered away in French.

*"De quoi parlez-vous, mes enfants?"*

"It's too hard to explain in French, Madame."

*"Non, non jamais. Expliquez, chère Sarah. Que se passe-t-il?"*

"Uh . . ." How could she explain all about the Kennedy pin, the shepherds, the angels. Oh, why did the most sympathetic ear in the school have to require French? "Well," Sarah began, *"Je suis un garde des moutons."*

"What!" Madame wheeled around still holding the chalk in her hand.

*"Un garde des moutons*—you know, a shepherd, Madame."

*"Une bergère . . ."* Mme. Henri said. "Oooh, that domb Christmas pageant again!" she muttered. Madame had a way of saying the word *dumb* in English that made the thing sound even dumber than it actually was. *"Continuez, chérie."*

6

"Well, *j'ai porté une robe et un chapeau orné d'un bouton Kennedy.*"

"*Ah! Ça c'est charmant, Sarah!*" exclaimed Madame.

"Not so *charmant,*" Elaine and Sarah said in unison. Everyone laughed.

"*Qu'est-ce qui est arrivé?*"

What happened, Sarah translated to herself. "Well, *Mademoiselle Crowninshield était furieuse.*"

"Oooh la la! Mademoiselle Crowninshield." Madame turned to the board and began writing.

To this point, most of the writing on the blackboard constituted food words. Madame Henri loved to cook and eat, although her figure was quite trim. A favorite assignment of hers for the junior high French students was that of making up French menus, especially at holiday time. The walls of the classroom were decorated with menus from famous Paris restaurants. Now, however, she was writing all the French words for angry: *en colère, fâché, furieux.*

*En colère. Je suis en colère* over the Christmas pageant, Sarah thought as she drove home with Marla after school. How many more rehearsals could she take? They were winding down a narrow suburban road, passing stately colonial homes that appeared bleak in the thin November sun.

"Three," Marla said.

"Three what?"

"That is the third little black stable-boy statue on this road." She pointed to a small figure of a black-faced man in cap and breeches extending his hand at the end of a driveway. "That is so offensive," Marla sighed. "Imagine if you were a black person how you'd feel if you drove past these fancy houses and saw a statue that

7

reeks of racism. 'Comin' with yo' julep, Massa. Jus' let me take yo' horse, Massa!' "

"I would be *en colère* if I were colored."

"Sarah! Don't say *colored*. Say *black*."

"Mom and Dad say *Negro*."

"Well, people are starting to say *black* now."

"Well, I'm glad Mom and Dad don't have a black stable-boy statue."

"Are you crazy? They never would."

"I'm glad they don't have a flamingo either."

"Who has a flamingo?"

"I don't know, but I've seen them on people's lawns."

"Well, Mom and Dad are neither morally nor socially tacky, so don't lose sleep over it."

Sarah wasn't sure exactly what Marla meant by "morally or socially tacky." Marla was terribly smart. So smart that sometimes Sarah didn't understand her.

They were now approaching their own neighborhood. Sarah saw only one stable-boy statue. The lawns were not just "manicured" but "established." Last spring Sarah had heard their landscape man say that. She supposed it meant that the trees and bushes were big and old and luxuriant. The lawns were not like the ones north of Seventy-first Street in those developments that had ridiculously romantic names like Tara Hills and Sweetwater Estates. One could hardly call those lawns. They were really grass-carpeted plots punctuated with teensy little stiff shrubs and frail saplings. No, in Sarah's neighborhood there were big copper beeches, oaks, maples, dogwoods, flowering crabtrees, and no romantic names.

They passed several one-story colonial-style houses—brick, with eagle fixtures over their front doors—and then a few two- and three-story homes made of stone and crowned with round turrets and what Sarah called witch-hat roofs. The Benjamins lived in one of these. Sarah's room was a twentieth-century scaled-down turret. It was the smallest bedroom in the house, but it was hers by choice. Its curved wall encircled her, and its witch-hat roof perched overhead. She could not, of course, see the shape of the witch's hat when she was in her bedroom. But she could feel it.

# Chapter Two

Sarah and her sister sat at the Formica counter in the kitchen doing their homework to the pounding cadences of their mother hammering veal cutlets into tenderness. Marla had just finished translating eight pages of Virgil. Sarah was up to the entrée on her French menu for Thanksgiving. She was using a broad-nibbed calligraphy pen and doing her best to make it look as nice as the writing on Madame's *Tour d'Argent* menu.

Marla looked over. "Sarah, that's lovely, but do you realize that you're writing it on the back of the postoperative instructions that Dad gives his face-lift patients?"

"Oh, *yeccch!* Sarah!" Their mother stopped slamming the veal and turned around.

"I like this pink color. The breast-implant instructions are on that horrible orange color. It looks like it's from Howard Johnson's. Besides, this doesn't really show through that much."

"Let's see," said Marla. She held the paper up to the light.

"Well, if you hold it like that it does," Sarah said.

"Look," said Marla, flipping the paper over. "Right here under your appetizer, just below *'moules à la marinière,'* it says 'No chewing for two or three days—liquids only.' "

"Mussels don't require much chewing," Sarah offered. "They just sort of slide down."

"And look, right under your entrée: 'Avoid any activity that might stretch the facial skin or muscles and pull the stitches loose.' "

Marla continued reading. " 'No hair grooming for five days after surgery and then only with a large-tooth comb. Rule number four: No makeup. Number five: No exposure to sun unless heavy creams are used.' "

"Well, I'll mount it on some construction paper. It will never show."

There was a stomping sound outside the back door. "Dad's home," Shirley Benjamin said. A blast of cold air streamed in. The pink menu fluttered in Marla's hands.

"Hi, gang!" A portly man entered.

"You look like Frosty the Snowman," said Sarah. The fringe of wiry hair visible just under the brim of Alfred Benjamin's hat was indeed frosted white with snow.

"It's really coming down out there. How's my girls?"

"Rotten."

"Great."

"Rotten—why, Sarah? Great—I won't probe, Marla. Leave well enough alone. Hi, honey." He kissed his wife. He took off his coat and put it on the counter.

Shirley Benjamin picked it up. "Hang up your coat, Alf. You know, for a surgeon you really are a slob at home. You're supposed to be compulsive."

"Well, aren't you glad I limit it to the operating room?"

"Yes," Sarah said. "Elaine's father is terrible. Their whole house is like an operating room."

"So why are you so rotten, kiddo?"

"Because—" Sarah paused dramatically. "You are not going to believe this."

"Try me," her father said. He was tired, his voice drenched with exhaustion.

"I haven't even told you, Mom."

11

"Do I need a drink to hear this?" her father asked.

"No, but you're still not going to believe it."

"Yes?" said her dad.

"Well, guess what Crowninshield chewed me out for today?"

"What?" her parents asked in unison. Her mother's pixieish face was alert.

"You know what a burnoose is?"

"Yeah, one of those head things Arabs wear," Shirley said.

"And you know that I am a shepherd in the Christmas pageant, as I was last year?"

"Yeah, yeah," her father said. "So what happened?"

"I wore this"—Sarah pointed to her Kennedy pin—"on my burnoose during rehearsal and Miss Crowninshield had a fit."

"You're kidding." For a fraction of a second there was a bewildered look in Alf Benjamin's eyes. Sarah knew that he wouldn't really disapprove. Then a smile broke across his face. "That's cute. I wish I had been there." He hugged her. "Oh, Sarah, you're so adorable!" Shirley was smiling, too.

Something inside of Sarah deflated. "It wasn't cute, Dad. I am not *adorable*. Miss Crowninshield does not think I am adorable. I got into trouble."

"It was a political statement, which is fine: a shepherd wearing a campaign button in the Nativity scene," Marla said.

"It wasn't even that," Sarah said. "How do I know which party shepherds voted for in Bethlehem back then?"

Alf Benjamin compressed his lips to keep from laughing again, at the same time savoring every word his younger daughter was saying. "You know, Shirley, they don't appreciate Sarah enough there." He shook his head. "Despite what you think, Sarah, that *is* truly adorable." Why didn't she feel great? Her parents thought she was adorable. Did they think Kennedy was adorable, too?

12

"I know what you're going to say, Alf: Sarah should switch schools. Sarah knows she can go to the public school whenever she wants. But she doesn't want to."

"All my friends are at Stuart Hall. I've been there since the second grade. It's just that this pageant starts to get me."

"Me, too," Marla said. "Thank heavens this is the last year I have to play the piano for it."

"Maybe they have pageants in college," Sarah said.

"If they do I'm sure they're an elective, and I shall elect not to be an accompanist for them."

"I hate being a shepherd. I'm doomed to being one for four more years."

"Look at Yul Brynner," her father offered as he poured some Scotch over ice cubes. "He's been the King of Siam for years now."

"It's more fun being a king than being a shepherd, and he gets paid, too."

"Well, there are those three kings in the pageant. Maybe you could get a king part," Alf said hopefully.

"You have to be able to sing to get those roles," Marla told him.

"I wish I could be an angel." Sarah sounded wistful.

"You are an angel, darling. A slightly kooky angel."

Shirley scratched her head. "I can't say that I would be entirely comfortable with you as an angel in the pageant. After all, we are Jewish."

"There could be Jewish angels, couldn't there?" Alf said.

"I don't know." Shirley put a scallop of veal in the frying pan. "You're the one who got bar mitzvahed. But frankly, I wouldn't consider it an appropriate role for a Jewish girl. You know, Marla's playing the piano is fine. It isn't religiously compromising. She's just making beautiful music."

"What am I making as a shepherd?"

"Oh, Sarah!" Shirley laughed.

"Well, is being a shepherd an appropriate role for a Jewish girl?"

"Ah-ha!" Alf pointed his finger at Shirley. "She's got you there, Shirley!"

"Well, I'm sure there were Jewish shepherds. We weren't all moneylenders, pharisees, and scribes. I'm sure there were a few, you know, who could have been shepherds with, uh . . ." Shirley was tearing up leaves of romaine lettuce.

"Sheep," Sarah said.

"Yes. Exactly. So just think of it, Sarah. You are helping to break down a stereotype of Jews as scribes and moneylenders by being a shepherd."

Sarah rolled her eyes. "You know, Mom, it's lucky that I'm a very stable adolescent. Because if I weren't, I could really have a trauma over being the younger sister of a musical prodigy whose mother has just told her that she is making a major contribution to human understanding by being a shepherd in a Christmas pageant."

Shirley turned around slowly. Under her thick bangs of red hair her bright blue eyes were rimmed with tears. Her mouth was clamped shut. Sarah wasn't sure whether her mother was about to laugh or cry.

"Oh, Sarah." Shirley sighed. "You're ten zillion times smarter than your mother. You don't have to be a shepherd or anything else, because you're you. And I swear you are the most totally unique creature on the face of the earth."

Sarah knew her mother meant this as a compliment, but at this stage in her life being told that she was different was not very comforting.

"Well, Mom, don't worry about the angels," Marla said.

"They only choose blondes with very straight hair and blue eyes."

"Really?" Shirley looked up. "How peculiar. Do they really think . . ." A funny little smile began to break across her face.

"They? You mean Christians?" Sarah said.

"Yes. Do you suppose they think that angels only have blonde hair and blue eyes?"

"Naw," Marla said. "It's Crowninshield mostly."

"Here," said Shirley, handing Marla the salad bowl. "Toss this and take it to the table."

Marla began tossing the salad. "I actually don't dare imagine what Crowninshield's requirements for the Virgin Mary are."

"Sarah, you could help, too, you know," Shirley said. "Carry in that casserole."

"How can you ask me to carry in a noodle casserole when I am writing *médaillons de veau au vin*?"

"We are having medallions of voh, only without the van," Shirley said, pointing to the veal scallops.

"Oh Lord!" Alf groaned. "And you're writing it on the back of my face-lift instructions. That's nauseating."

"Dad, you're so squeamish for a surgeon." Sarah carefully drew a triangular dot for the *i* in *vin*. "After all, it's all tissue, doc! Ho-ho-ho!"

"You're disgusting, Sarah!" Marla scowled.

The family was seated. Alf Benjamin had just finished his first bite of veal.

"Good tissue, Shirley."

"Alf!"

"Now we know where she gets it, Mom," Marla said.

"So tomorrow's the big day," Alf said. "What do the latest polls say?"

"Walter Cronkite said on the news tonight it's going to be very close," Shirley said, shoveling a small mountain of noodle casserole onto Marla's plate.

"That's too much, Mom."

"No it isn't."

"Come on, Mom. I don't burn that many calories."

"Those Chopin études burn them like crazy. You were practicing all afternoon."

"When is the recital, Marla?" her father asked.

"Sunday."

"It's the Friends of the Symphony who sponsor this, right? And you're doing the harp étude?"

"Yeah and yeah."

"How's it going?"

Marla lifted her hand and waggled it horizontally over her noodles in a "so-so" gesture.

"I think Kennedy's going to win," Sarah said abruptly. "A feeling in my bones. Won't Aunt Hattie be ecstatic? Too bad she can't vote."

"Can't vote!" the other three shouted.

"Of course she can vote." Shirley turned to her daughter. "You don't think Hattie would miss a chance to vote for John Kennedy? She sent her ballot in weeks ago."

"From London?" Sarah asked.

"Where have you been for the last thirteen years, Sarah?" Marla asked. "Haven't you ever heard of an absentee ballot?"

"Well, I didn't realize you could do it out of the country."

"Of course, dear," said her mother.

"How's Vronsky's tour going?" Alf asked.

"I guess fine. According to Hattie, he's kept his weight down and isn't doing too much nightlife."

"What's he dancing, *Swan Lake?*"

*"Swan Lake!"* the three female Benjamins cried.

"Alfred." Shirley took a sip of water. "Serge Vronsky hasn't danced *Swan Lake* in years."

"That tub of lard dance *Swan Lake?*" Sarah said.

"Sarah!" Shirley spoke sharply. "That was cruel."

"Sorry," Sarah said meekly.

"No," Shirley said, turning to Alf, "he's doing *Romeo and Juliet* and *Sleeping Beauty*. Not so strenuous but still enough opportunity to show his virtuoso quality. He's getting standing ovations and Hattie is very pleased with the tour. He opened last night in Covent Garden. I think it was a command performance."

"If John Kennedy gets elected, maybe Vronsky will be asked to dance at the White House," Marla suggested.

"Won't Hattie love that." Shirley smiled. "Oh, I just remembered. Hattie sent all the way from London a box of those wonderful Fortnum and Mason cookies."

The girls made sounds of delight.

"Hattie has her redeeming qualities," Marla added.

"What do you mean, redeeming qualities, Marla?" Shirley said in a perplexed tone. "Hattie is my sister and although not flawless is a wonderful and talented woman. I should be half so successful."

"Well, she's successful. But I don't exactly know what you mean by talented."

"Marla." Shirley turned to her elder daughter and looked directly into her eyes. "You are a talented pianist. Talent, granted, is usually associated with observable artistic skills, but, believe me, being a manager of artistic talent is a talent, too. We all know that Serge Vronsky is no piece of cake to manage. Neither is that Lila Podhoretz, or any of the musicians, dancers, and artists that Hattie has handled."

17

"If she had been a man," Alf said, "she would have been as famous as Sol Hurok."

"Exactly," said Shirley. "She was the first female impresario and is still the most distinguished. It's just that there are more people doing it now and some of her artists are, well"—Shirley paused—"getting on."

"It shouldn't matter with musicians," Marla said. "Look at Arthur Rubinstein, Pablo Casals—well past seventy and going strong."

"Well," said Shirley, "she had a few bad breaks. It wasn't her fault that Lila Podhoretz drank herself into oblivion. Oh gads, will you ever forget that last Carnegie Hall appearance when she fell off the piano bench?"

"Listen," said Alf. "Lila Podhoretz wasn't her only bad break. That crazy Indian musician! Remember when he was calling me almost every week? He wanted a face-lift, then a blepharoplasty—and for nothing!"

"Why a blepharoplasty?" Shirley asked. "His eyelids were fine. He had gorgeous eyes."

"He also wanted a hair transplant and a lipectomy," Alf continued.

"A lipectomy? All he needed was to lose twenty pounds and those chins would have melted away," Shirley said.

"He was talking a hundred thousand dollars' worth of plastic surgery."

"Well, he spent five thousand dollars on his teeth, and Hattie wound up paying that."

"You should give Vronsky a butt tuck," Sarah said.

"What's wrong with his butt?" Shirley asked.

"Oh, Mom, in his tights it's just too fat. It really sticks out. Remember last winter in Chicago when he was dancing *Les Sylphides?*"

"Listen," Alf Benjamin said, "with all your little jibes at Serge Vronsky, he is one of the most decent fellows I know. He would never consider asking me for free surgery or pumping me for advice as have some of Hattie's other clients. He is a gentleman and a great dancer."

"Was," whispered Marla.

"He still is!" Shirley rapped the table with her fingers for emphasis.

When they had finished dinner and cleared the table, Marla went to the piano and began practicing the Chopin étude. Sarah finished her math homework and wrote two book reports, one on *Johnny Tremain,* the other on *Giants in the Earth,* which she had sobbed her way through the previous weekend. She had to think now about a research project for social studies. It could be about anything, but it had to include survey techniques (direct interview or questionnaire forms), simple graphs, and a written description of the project. All the good topics had been taken. Elaine was doing a research project in the kindergarten–first grade on what five- and six-year-olds knew or thought about the current presidential election. (Not much. It would be an easy report.) Lucy Nyles was doing a survey of the nutritional habits of six American families who lived in her neighborhood. (Excruciatingly boring.) Lisa Cody, who was Lucy's best friend and had never had an original idea in her life, was doing the exercise habits of six American families who lived in her neighborhood. Sarah had thought about doing a project that involved politics or movies or movie stars. She loved going to movies and followed movie stars' lives in fan magazines. But she couldn't figure out anything to ask movie stars in a research project. She sat at her desk and chewed on her pencil.

The notes of the Chopin étude drifted in from the living room where Marla practiced. Marla had struggled all afternoon with the left-hand stretches, which were particularly troublesome in this piece. Now she had begun to master them, and the legato was melodious and becoming smooth as silk. The sounds came shimmering and fragile. Like great bubbles they floated through the house, over the oriental rugs, over the sounds of the television show in the den where Perry Mason pleaded the defendant's case as her father snoozed and her mother read. Shirley would awaken Alf when the true culprit broke down and confessed. Sarah yawned and remembered not to yelp, her usual style of finishing a yawn. It was such a release, but she did not want to shatter the gorgeous bubbles of music.

Except for the fact that she was a shepherd and she could not think of a research project, life was okay, she realized suddenly, with her sister playing music and her parents relaxing in front of the TV. Nobody was compulsive in her family—surgically or otherwise. There were no curfews, no rules about homework or telephone calls. Marla was the smartest, most talented girl at Stuart Hall. But she was never stuck-up. She looked out for Sarah: helped her with homework, lent her clothes, was nice to her friends. Things were just fine as they were, Sarah thought as she walked back to her bedroom after kissing her parents good-night, and by this time tomorrow night Kennedy might be president!

"Marla!" Sarah jiggled her sister's shoulder. "Wake up, Marla! It's important!"

"What?" Marla muttered.

"I've got to turn on your light. Close your eyes."

"Ohhh." Marla groaned as the small bedside lamp, an electrically wired bust of Mozart, flared brightly beneath its shade. "Sarah, it's three o'clock in the morning! What is it?"

"Marla, I've had an inspiration."

"Can't it wait until morning?"

"Marla, I thought you'd want to be the first to know because I've bothered you so much about my research project."

"Well, I certainly don't want to be bothered about it at three in the morning. Look, I told you I'd think of a topic for you by Friday. Just cool it."

"You don't have to think of one, Marla! You're off the hook. I've thought of one!"

"Sarah! Honestly, I don't *believe* you. You wake me in the middle of the night to tell me you've thought of a research project topic so you won't have to bother me anymore. Doesn't that strike you as slightly illogical—bothering me to tell me you won't have to bother me?"

"Oh dear!" Sarah sighed. "Well, I was just so excited."

"Okay," Marla said, hiking herself up onto her elbow. Her hair hung in a tangle over her right ear. Her delicate oval face looked pale, except for her longish nose, which was pink as a rabbit's and running slightly. "What is this great project?"

"Angel Perception Analysis. APA."

"Whaaat?" Marla's russet eyebrows slid toward each other and joined in a knot.

"Okay, remember what we were talking about tonight in the kitchen? Crowninshield's theory of angelness—blonde, blue-eyed?"

"Yeah, yeah," Marla nodded.

"Well— Oh, this is so neat you won't believe it." Sarah scrambled onto the end of Marla's bed. "*That* is Crowninshield's view. But how do you suppose other people perceive angels? Other people like for instance Martin Luther King. Do you think he pictures blonde-haired, blue-eyed angels, or Rosa Parks or . . ."

Marla reached for her glasses by the Mozart lamp. She put them on and peered intently at her younger sister. "Are you serious, Sarah?"

21

Was it Sarah's imagination, or did she detect a quiet flush of jubilation rising within Marla? "You're darned right I'm serious," Sarah whispered conspiratorially. "I intend to do a study of how prominent Americans perceive angels. I'm going to make up a questionnaire complete with a chart of hair, eye, and skin colors. They can circle the appropriate shades to indicate their choices."

"Which Americans?" Marla asked.

"Well, as I said, Martin Luther King, Rosa Parks, John Kennedy of course, and I think I've got to include an astronaut. And then I thought maybe Walt Disney for a change of pace. Besides, I think he might have some interesting ideas; and I'll also choose a movie star, say John Wayne, and the mayor of Indianapolis."

"The mayor of Indianapolis? Why, in heaven's name?"

"The homey touch, local color, you know. I was thinking about the pope, too."

"He's hardly local. Or American, for that matter."

"I know, but I might make an exception because it would really be interesting to see how living in the Vatican, having the Sistine Chapel in your own home, affects your perception of angels."

"It's not as if he sleeps, eats, and watches TV in the Sistine Chapel," said Marla.

"Yeah, but there's got to be angels painted all over the joint, not just in the chapel."

"Well, Sarah, this is truly original!"

"I know. I'm so excited I can hardly wait to start making up the questionnaire."

"Don't just rush into it. You have to make up your protocol first."

"Protocol? What's that?" Sarah asked.

"Your method of inquiry. How you intend to go about getting your information. And you have to have a statement of purpose, too, and most important you have to have a very good letter explaining your project to the participant or would-be participant so he or she won't think you're totally nuts. You can't just send a color chart to John Kennedy, especially if he's just been elected, and say 'Mr. President, please check an item in each column.' "

"Oh dear!" Sarah's face crumpled. "I'll never be able to write a convincing letter. Oh, Marla, would you help? Just an opening sentence?"

Marla sank back against her pillow. "I will. You know it. But wasn't it just three days ago that I gave you an opening sentence for your report on the Ice Age and you promised it was the last one you would ever ask for?"

"I know, I know. But it's just opening sentences I need. Once I get one I'm off and running."

"What are you going to do next year when I'm at college?"

"Uh, I don't know."

"Listen, go back to bed. It's nearly dawn. I'll help you with the letter, but not now."

Sarah tried not to think about Marla's going to college. It did seem paradoxical to Sarah that it was her own journey without her sister, not Marla's, that seemed full of peril. She thought of herself in the same way that fifteenth-century people must have thought of Columbus—a lone voyager who would drop off the edge of a flat world.

# Chapter Three

"Good morning, students," the crisp voice of Miss Crownin-shield piped over the public address system as morning announcements commenced and were broadcast into the homeroom classes of Stuart Hall. "Today is election day. As the country goes to the polls, we here at Stuart Hall have our own business to pursue. Pageant rehearsal today shall be third period, beginning promptly at ten-fifteen." Sarah winced as she stood with two other people waiting to make announcements. It seemed to Sarah that while the rest of the country went to the polls Stuart Hall did indeed march to a different beat. There were the usual "reminders," small commands aimed at keeping Stuart Hall an orderly and productive environment conducive to study: no running in the halls, no splitting Oreo cookies at lunch, no talking during rehearsals—"Shepherds, that means you! And now we have some other announcements. Amy Phillips, please."

A thin senior with straggly black hair stepped up to the public-address microphone. "If anybody has seen a critique about 'Ode to a Grecian Urn' with my name on it, please get it to me. I think it fell out of my notebook someplace between the hockey field and the parking lot."

"Organization, Amy!" Miss Crowninshield chimed in. "Organization! We must be orderly with our papers."

Oh shut up, Sarah thought. The poor girl has lost her paper. Don't make her feel worse!

24

"Miss Forest next."

Miss Forest, a squat woman with hair like scrambled eggs and the charm of a marine drill sergeant, stepped up. "I have a list of overdue books here. I'm getting tired of this, and that goes for you: Adams—*Silas Marner;* Kitchen—*The Good Earth;* Hartley—*Tess of the d'Urbervilles;* Wheeler—*The Jubilee Trail;* Nutting—*The Witch of Blackbird Pond;* Rogers—*The Red Badge of Courage;* Cummings— *Victory at Salamis.* I want those in," Miss Forest barked, "on the double!"

"Thank you, Miss Forest." Miss Crowninshield then sighed so deeply that, amplified by the public address system, it must have sounded, Sarah thought, as if she were inhaling entire homerooms. "This is sloppy behavior. Irresponsible. One cannot go through life being overdue. And now Sarah Benjamin has an announcement."

Sarah took a deep breath. "Yeah. Uh, I'd like to say that for a research project that I am working on I need pictures of those Breck shampoo hair girls. So if anybody finds any in old magazines and would tear them out and bring them to me, I would really appreciate it. Uh, that's all . . . thank you."

Sarah returned to her eighth-grade classroom. Mrs. Thomas was their main teacher; but first period was math, so Miss Wardlow was there. Sarah was terrible in math. For the past week they had been working on square roots and common denominators. Sarah had a theory. There were certain things in life that certain people would never be able to do, for instance figuring square roots, playing Brahms concertos, and, say, wrestling alligators. So why knock your brains out? It would not mean that you would not survive. You just had to be quicker in other ways and find alternative methods. Nobody had ever died of not being able to do a square root. This Sarah knew. So she stopped listening to Miss Wardlow and started writing her statement of purpose for her social-studies project.

"The purpose of the Angel Perception Analysis is to study how people think they should look." Sarah reread her first sentence. She had to think of classier words, more scientific words. She chewed her pencil and stared blankly ahead. Miss Wardlow was doing an incredibly long square root. It cascaded from the top of the blackboard almost to the chalk tray. Sarah crossed out the word *think* and she thought. It's not really so much *think* as *visualize*—that was the word! She whispered it to herself, then rewrote the last part of the sentence: "how people visualize angels. By this study I hope to gain some knowledge of people's ideas and their prejudices." Again she stopped. There must be some better words for "knowledge" and "prejudices." "Prejudices" sounded kind of strong. Mrs. Thomas might not want to read her project if she saw the word *prejudice* in the first paragraph. Suddenly Sarah was aware that every head in the classroom was turned toward her.

"Sarah!" Miss Wardlow's voice came as if out of a distant canyon. "Are you with us, Sarah Benjamin?" she called.

"Oh! Sorry!"

"Sarah, it's no use being sorry. Now, I ask you what happens when we get to this point in taking the square root of 891,572?"

Sarah felt a rising tide of confusion. What point were they at? What in the heck was Miss Wardlow talking about? "I don't know." Sarah's answer was barely more than a whisper.

"Sarah, were you following?"

"Uh, I guess not."

"Sarah, this attitude will get you nowhere."

*Attitude!* That was the word she needed. She could cross out *prejudices* and put in *attitude*.

For second period, language arts and English literature, Mrs. Thomas came back to the room. Sarah liked this. They learned how to diagram predicate adjectives, then discussed the concept of "word color" in "The Highwayman." Sarah loved the poem. She would have loved to be Bess, the landlord's daughter, although she found it a bit difficult to imagine that she could have actually killed herself to warn the highwayman, as Bess had done when she had been tied up with the musket to her chest. Miss Thomas had a beautiful reading voice:

"He'd a French cocked-hat on his forehead, a bunch of
      lace at his chin
A coat of the claret velvet, and breeches of brown doe-
      skin;
They fitted with never a wrinkle; his boots were up to
      the thigh!
And he rode with a jeweled twinkle
His pistol butts a-twinkle,
      His rapier hilt a-twinkle, under the jeweled sky.
      Over the cobbles he clattered and clashed in the
      dark inn-yard,
And he tapped with his whip on the shutters, but all
      was locked and barred;
He whistled a tune to the window, and who should be
      waiting there
But the landlord's black-eyed daughter,
Bess, the landlord's daughter,
Plaiting a dark red love-knot into her long black hair."

Sarah flew with the rolling cadences, her eyes rapt with attention as she followed Mrs. Thomas's reading. The teacher looked up
and smiled. "You like that one, don't you, Sarah? What is it you
like so much?"

"Well——" Sarah thought. "It kind of moves, you know. At
least compared to that poem 'Snowbound' by Whittier. I mean, it

was a nice poem, but it kind of . . ." Sarah didn't know how to put it. "Well, you know, there's that line in 'Snowbound' about how they roasted the apples."

" 'Apples sputtering in a row,' " Mrs. Thomas offered.

"Yeah, that's the one. Well, that's sort of the way the whole poem is—uh, cozy and sputtering." The other girls laughed. "Well, it doesn't actually sputter—the poem."

"I think I know what Sarah means," Mrs. Thomas said helpfully. "It's the tone of the poem that Sarah is talking about. We've talked about tone and mood and characterization, girls. *Coziness* is an appropriate word here, for a poem like 'Snowbound.' But what would you say is the tone of 'The Highwayman,' Sarah?"

Sarah hesitated. "Moonlight and movement, I guess."

"Yes! Yes! Now, remember the Robert Frost poem 'Swinger of Birches'? It had a lot of movement in it. Did you like that one too, Sarah?"

"It's okay."

All brain activity ground to a halt, of course, in third-period pageant rehearsal. The slumbering heap reassembled, this time with Sarah squashed between Phoebe Buxton and Hillary Daniels. Rehearsal ended at ten forty-five. The word spread like wildfire during recess: In the East the election outcome appeared to be a Democratic landslide. Marla was so excited that she came down to the junior wing, unheard of for an upperclassman (except if one were the sole Democrat in the senior class), to rejoice with Sarah and Elaine, the only two Democrats in the eighth grade. Marla's best friend, Suzanne Elkins, accompanied her. "Don't count your chickens before they hatch, Marla," said Suzanne. "After all, it's noon in the East, but in California it's nine in the morning."

By early afternoon Eastern Standard Time, Kennedy had 272 electoral votes. He needed only three more, but Nixon's popular vote was closing in fast. Marla and Sarah drove the usual route home from school. They listened to the car radio as the election results continued to come in from the western states. Tomorrow this time, Sarah thought, if Kennedy won, nothing would have changed, exactly. The stable-boy statues would still be there. Every substantial home, filled with substantial civic-minded Republicans, would be unchanged. And yet, it would all be different. There was with Kennedy this challenge, this promise of adventure, that had nothing to do with well-maintained homes and manicured lawns. There was this notion of "pioneers" heading toward a "frontier." But the frontier wasn't history anymore: It was alive. Kennedy wanted to put a man in space. And he wanted a corps of young people to go out all over the globe to help the sick, the starving, and the illiterate. If he won, thought Sarah, as they passed another ceramic stable boy, by tomorrow that statue is going to be smiling for entirely different reasons.

Shirley served dinner on TV tables in the den. By eight o'clock Alf was ready to break out the champagne.

"I don't think we should," Shirley cautioned. "Nixon hasn't conceded yet."

"Well, I'm beat. I'm not staying up all night."

"We are," Marla and Sarah said at once. "Can we, Mom?"

"Sure. This is history."

"Well, I'm going to have to sleep through this part of history." Alf sighed.

The phone rang. Shirley got up to answer it. "You're not going to sleep through history. It's the hospital."

"Must be serious. I'm not on call tonight." Alf walked over to the telephone and took the receiver. "Yeah . . . yeah." Alf's face grew grim. "What caliber? Any major blood vessels severed? . . . Okay, I'll be right down." He hung up.

"Oh no." Shirley groaned.

29

"Oh yeah." Alf sat down and pulled off his slippers and put on his shoes.

"What is it, Dad?" Sarah asked.

"Gunshot," Alf said shortly. "Some guy's face blown half away. When are we going to get a handgun law in this country? This is the third gunshot wound I've been called in on this week." Alf arose heavily and went for his coat.

Sarah had fallen asleep on the couch. It was after midnight.

"Michigan, Texas, he's got them." Marla was shaking her shoulder.

"Huh?" Sarah blinked. A kind of jubilant white noise was pouring from the television, and a lot of people with hats and banners were jumping up and down.

"He's got them, Sarah. Michigan and Texas are Kennedy's!"

Sarah sat up and rubbed her eyes. Her French grammar and a sheet of irregular-verb conjugations slipped to the floor. "Did Nixon concede?"

"Not yet," Marla said. "Wait a minute! Wait! Wait!"

"And now," the television announcer was saying, "we are going to switch to the Ambassador Hotel in Los Angeles, the Nixon headquarters where our West Coast anchorman John Billings is. . . . John, can you hear us?"

"Yes, Walter. I am waiting here in the main ballroom of the Ambassador, where hundreds of disappointed Nixon supporters are gathered. We have just had a report that the Vice President and Mrs. Nixon are on their way." There was a pause. "Here they come. I see them coming now. They are making their way to the podium. We have not been given any indication that this is to be a concession speech. Mr. Nixon looks somber, but quite composed. His wife, Pat—Mrs. Nixon—does appear slightly more agitated. Yes, I think

30

that you can see as that camera moves in close she seems quite devastated, but yet always there is that dignity."

The crowds quieted. Nixon had begun to speak. Marla and Sarah sat on the couch. They clutched each other's hands.

"I am afraid," Nixon started, "if the present trend continues . . ."

"Present trend continues! What is he talking about?" Sarah exclaimed. "The electoral votes are all in!"

"Never say die," Marla muttered.

"We can only try to let you know what's in our hearts." Nixon spoke in a rough voice.

"This is definitely a concession speech. I declare it so," Marla said.

"Marla, are you serious?"

The station then cut to Hyannis Port, Massachusetts. The din of jubilation, of victory in the Kennedy camp, poured from the television. Glimpses of Kennedys with their thick, unruly hair and incredible energy flashed across the screen. Sarah could hardly believe it. Most of her life the president had been a bald, kindly man who played golf. Now, here was all this energy. It was infectious. The final electoral figures flashed across the screen. She and Marla leaped from the couch. They howled and hugged each other. Sarah picked up her heavier sister. "We won! We won! You weigh a ton!" She dropped Marla with a thud and spun off into a little victory jig on her homework papers, fittingly the irregular French verbs. Marla, caught up in the spirit, danced out of the den toward the living room. The daisies on her flannel nightgown jumped around. She sat down at the piano and played a jazz improvisation of "America the Beautiful."

As Marla played, Sarah thought that it was beautiful, everything was beautiful in a boundaryless way. Every space that Sarah had known had been cultivated, landscaped. Her environment was filled with carefully pruned shrubbery, school playing fields, golf courses, and shopping centers. But now, beyond all that, there was this new frontier, a wilderness for true pioneers.

"We need food! Food for the new frontiersmen." Sarah boogied toward the kitchen.

"Frontierswomen!" Marla yelled.

Sarah climbed up on the counter. It was against her principles to use stepladders. She reached for the tin of Fortnum and Mason cookies. She grabbed two Cokes from the refrigerator on her way out of the kitchen. Marla had finished her piano playing. Sarah began taking the lid off the ivory-colored tin box. It was a beautiful box with embossed roses and eighteenth-century powder-wigged ladies and gentlemen. She crooned as she peered down at the array of tiny cookies installed in the orderly paper compartments. "What'll it be? Lemon Crisp, Matinee Wafer, Hebridean Cream, Scottish Shortbread, or a Jewel of the Punjab?"

They munched cookies and drank their Cokes and talked into the night. Sarah would always remember it as the night of greatest promise, and she felt she was part of that promise.

# Chapter Four

Four hours later, at half past six, the phone rang.

"Hattie!" Through her bedroom door, through the goose-down quilt pulled up around her head, Sarah could hear her mother's transatlantic squawk. Shirley Benjamin's voice rose two octaves and countless decibels whenever she talked to her sister Hattie, especially if there was an ocean between them. "Yes! I know he won. . . . Yes, isn't it exciting. . . . Quite close, yes. The popular vote was unbelievably close. . . . Serge is excited, too? . . . I bet. Where are you all staying? . . . The Connaught? Oh good, darling. Do you have the peach-colored room? . . . Oh lovely. How's Serge doing? What's he dancing? . . . A lot of royalty? . . . You're kidding. Oh no! . . . The girls are great. . . . Yeah. Marla plays this weekend. Clowes Hall. . . . I know the acoustics are lousy. *They* know the acoustics are lousy, so what can you do? . . . The harp étude. . . . Gorgeous. Sarah's adorable as always. Alf's at the hospital. He's been there all night. . . . Okay, darling. . . . *Mwatch, mwatch!*" Shirley always closed her conversations with Hattie on a sound Sarah found utterly disgusting—a transatlantic kiss that sounded as if the wires had shredded on the ocean floor. Visions of strands of wire were transmuted to a tangle of chocolate-brown octopus arms as Sarah drifted back to sleep until the alarm restored routine.

When Sarah arrived in the kitchen her mother was trying to talk over the "Today Show" election report. "Hattie said that Princess Margaret looked absolutely ravishing and the Queen looked terrible, but Philip was gorgeous."

33

"The Queen wouldn't look so bad," Marla said, her eyes glued to the small television above the breakfast counter where she was eating her cereal, "if she'd use big rollers to set her hair instead of those skinny little ones. Look at Jackie; doesn't she look gorgeous?" Television cameras had just zeroed in on the soon-to-be First Lady. "See her hair—nice bouffant look."

"See her body," Sarah said. "Also bouffant."

"She's due any day," Shirley said.

"Where are my French verbs?" Sarah screamed suddenly.

"How should I know?" her mother replied.

"*Où se trouvent les verbes français de Sarah?*" Marla offered.

"Don't be funny, Marla! Where are my verbs? I have to find them. There's a test today. I have to study them."

"Didn't you study last night?" Shirley asked.

"No."

"Well, why not?"

"Mother!" Sarah sighed "History was being made. You want me to be studying irregular French verbs while American history is being made?"

"Well, eat your breakfast and then look for them."

"No. I can't eat until I find them."

"You must eat."

"I can't!"

"Shut up!" Marla yelled. "I can't hear Rose Kennedy."

"Oh!" Shirley and Sarah both swung their heads toward the television, but the interview with John Kennedy's mother was just ending.

"Sarah," Marla said, "what verbs were they?"

"Uh, let's see. There were two *ir* ones, *battir* and *finir,* and then there was *mettre* and another one I can't remember."

"Well, sit down, shut up, eat your breakfast, and I'll conjugate those for you."

34

"Everything? I mean all the tenses. Conditional future?"

"Yes." Marla reached for a piece of paper. "Just don't go having conniptions. It's no way to celebrate a victory."

Marla was right. She was standing at the edge of the New Frontier that Kennedy had been championing for the last year. How could she have arrived at this point having fits about irregular French verbs and an argument with her mother about eating breakfast? She silently ate her breakfast, listened to the television, and watched Marla. While Marla ate and watched TV, she conjugated *battir* in all nine tenses.

Sarah studied the verbs all the way to school. On Wednesdays, luckily, French was first period. She had only to keep these conjugations in her brain for a total of thirty-five minutes after leaving the house. This included the twenty-minute drive to school, five minutes for Mrs. Thomas's announcements in homeroom and ten minutes for Crowninshield's morning address. Oh yes, another minute to get to Madame's room.

She would conjugate all the verbs in the future conditional first, since that was her least favorite tense. But this morning it would be hard to keep it all in her head. Everybody would be talking about the election, which of course would be distracting. Somehow she would have to keep jubilation and conjugation in balance.

As soon as she walked into the classroom she realized that it might not be so difficult, after all. A thick gloom hovered over the twenty desks like a heavy low cloud. Mrs. Thomas sat with her nose buried in her grade record book. Small knots of girls grumbled together, their shoulders hunched. "My father says . . ." was frequently heard. Although Sarah could not catch the ends of these phrases, doubtless they involved some ominous prediction. Elaine flew like a joyful missile from the reference corner of the room toward Sarah's desk. Her eyes sparkled.

"What a day!" she exclaimed.

"It was hardly a landslide!" Lisa Cody sneered over her shoulder and turned back to the small group she was talking with.

"It's going to be hard to celebrate in this atmosphere," Sarah muttered as they walked to French class.

*"Bonjour, mes jeunes filles."* Mme. Henri greeted them, resetting an elaborate earring into her pierced earlobe as she spoke. *"C'est un jour très special, le triomphe de Kennedy. Ainsi, pas d'examen des verbes irréguliers."*

There was a slight time lapse as the class translated Madame's remarks and the impact registered.

"No test!" Elaine shouted. "Because of Kennedy?"

*"Exactement!"*

A chorus of yeas rang out.

"Well," said Lisa Cody. "That's the best thing about his victory so far."

*"Lisa, chérie!"* Madame said, making a face at the girl. *"Quelle idiote vous êtes."* Everybody giggled, including Lisa. Madame frequently called the girls idiots and imbeciles. They were as much terms of endearment as anything else. *"Alors, mes petites imbéciles,"* she continued. *"Les choses vont changer."*

Things are going to change, Sarah translated happily.


The response to Sarah's request for magazine pictures of Breck shampoo models was substantial though not overwhelming. She had enough material to make several questionnaires and had decided to open up the survey to include her own classmates and a few teachers in addition to "selected" members of the onstage pageantry: one angel, one king, two shepherds, Mary, and Joseph.

Elaine helped Sarah paste up the survey sheets one afternoon.

"Remember, Elaine, this is a blind test. A whole face cannot appear. Just a patch of hair from the photo, one eye, and a patch of skin for skin color."

"Maybe you should draw a zit on the patch of skin."

"Elaine, don't be ridiculous. Nobody, no matter what their race, color, or creed, imagines an angel with acne."

"Did you notice that none of these Breck girls have curly hair? Barely a wave."

"I know. That's why I got these."

"What?" Elaine looked up from the paper scrap of platinum hair she was pasting down.

"*Ebony* magazine. I had to get some black people's hair and skin."

"Well, everyone is going to choose this one," Elaine said, patting the patch of silky blonde hair, "the Lacey Denton special."

"You never can tell," Sarah said. "As Madame says, *les choses vont changer*." She was thinking about the statues of the black-faced stable boys.

Three weeks later, on a Friday night, Alf Benjamin stood at the head of the dinner table. In his right hand he held a glass of wine and recited the *kiddush,* the Sabbath prayer, in Hebrew. Two candles burned in their holders on a side table, above which hung a mirror. Sarah looked up and saw the reflection of her family: They were radiant with their joy, for it was time for another celebration. "Amen," Alf said. "And now, Marla, if I may amend slightly an old phrase: next year not only Jerusalem, next year Wellesley!"

"Here! Here!" Shirley lifted her glass jauntily.

Sarah felt something hot and dark deep in her stomach. The letter had come just that morning from Wellesley College. The early decision welcomed Marla to the class of 1965. Marla had wanted to go straightaway to Juilliard, but her parents had insisted that she not start off in a music school. After two years in a liberal arts school she could transfer. There was a wonderful pianist in Boston with whom she would study while she was at Wellesley. It was all settled now. This time next year, Sarah thought, Marla would be in college, the men and women of the New Frontier on the march. Where would she, Sarah Eloise Benjamin, be, she wondered. Not on the New Frontier. Nope, she'd be sleeping to stage right just outside of Bethlehem, looking toward a tinfoil star into a conditional future.

# PART II

## NOVEMBER 1961

# Chapter Five

" 'My soul doth magnify the Lord, and my spirit hath rejoiced in God my Saviour. For he hath regarded the low estate of his handmaiden.' " Miss Crowninshield paused. "Now, it is on that cue—'handmaiden'—that you must play your first chords, Louanne. Marla always came in right at that moment. Almost immediately, but pianissimo."

Missamarlo pianomissamarlo—the words tumbled playfully through Sarah's head. She whispered them to herself, feeling the soft sibilant wind of the sounds on her lips.

"Benjamin?" Elaine's voice came from somewhere around her knees. "Did you know that you're in the advanced Latin group?"

"You're kidding!"

"No, you're on the list. It's posted on the academic bulletin board."

"I'll never keep up."

"It's not that hard," Elaine said.

"Bauer, not for you, but for me it is. I still don't understand the ablative absolute."

"Miss Henshaw thinks you do."

"That's her failing, not mine. It's perfectly obvious I don't understand it."

"Buxton." The small, weary voice of Hillary came from the region of Sarah's head. "It's about your crook. It's sticking me in the shoulder."

"Really, Phoebe," Elaine said. "You've been a shepherd as long as any of us. You should be able to handle your crook better."

"Don't be so condescending, Bauer," Phoebe muttered.

"What do you mean, 'condescending'? I'm just asking you to keep your darned crook off of us!"

"Crook control!" whispered Sarah.

"Who's playing Mary today?" Elaine asked.

"Suzanne Phillips. Who else would it be?" Phoebe said.

"No. Suzanne's got mono. Didn't you hear?"

"It's Lacey Denton," Hillary said.

"Daniels, you have to be kidding—Denton?" Sarah gasped.

"Yes, Denton," Hillary replied. "Can't you see?"

"Not under that Virgin outfit. Those robes hide her face, and they haven't turned on the star full blast yet."

"Well, you'll see. It's Lacey herself."

"That's incredible! I wonder what Roger Haynes thinks of Lacey's role."

"Why?" asked Hillary.

"Why!" The other three shepherds nearly yelped in their astonishment.

"Let's just say," Sarah whispered, "that he knows another side of her—to put it delicately." Hillary's innocence, Sarah thought, was limitless.

"Yeah," Elaine said. "They're always parked over there on that little road near the main entrance to Crown Hill Cemetery— they probably go inside the grounds."

"No!" Now Sarah's eyes flew open in shock, and just at that moment the star lit up to full wattage. "That is crude! That is the most sickening thing I have ever heard? Spare me! Making out in a cemetery!"

"Gee!" said Hillary. "Maybe they do it by James Whitcomb Riley's tomb."

A giggle rippled through the heap of shepherds.

"The *poet*—James Whitcomb Riley?" Phoebe whispered. "Is that where he's buried?"

"Buxton!" the other three shepherds chorused.

"Buxton!" Sarah said. "Don't you know anything about Indiana history? Yes our most famous poet is buried there. Do you think she's gone to third base with him? With Haynes, that is, not Riley."

"Gross! Benjamin, you have a capacity for grossness not to be believed," Elaine said.

"Well, do you think she's gone to third base with Roger Haynes?"

"Where have you been, Benjamin? Elaine muttered. "Of course she has—and farther. That's what makes her present dramatic role slightly, uh, weird. You yourself said so."

"Third base and more at James Whitcomb Riley's grave. *Whew!*" Sarah whispered.

"Sliding into home plate reciting— What's that poem of his?" Elaine asked.

"Whose? Haynes's?" Hillary asked.

"No, you idiot. James Whitcomb Riley's."

"Oh no!" Sarah sighed. "Doing it to 'Little Orphant Annie'!"

" 'Little Orphant Annie's come to our house to stay' "— Elaine began to recite the poem in a syrupy whisper—" 'An' wash the cups and saucers up, and brush the crumbs away,/An' shoo the chickens off the porch, an' dust the hearth, an' sweep,/An' make the fire, an' bake the bread, an' earn her board-an'-keep'!"

The shepherd-heap had begun to convulse.

"Shepherds!" There was the solid thwack of the orthopedic shoes across the auditorium floor. "Shepherds!" Miss Crowninshield clutched the Bible, open to the Gospel of St. Luke, to her tartan bosom. "Sit up!" she ordered.

42

"Ouch!" Elaine yelled as Phoebe Buxton's crook hit her on the temple. Miss Crowninshield was not distracted. Her normally colorless face was contorted and red. "Now, what precisely is so amusing?"

Sarah felt a bubble of laughter inflate deep inside her, but not deep enough. Her shoulders began to shake as she imagined Lacey and Roger rounding third base behind Riley's tombstone. The first small, watery gurgle broke the surface, and then like a tidal wave it came. She felt herself caught in the undertow of hysteria. Miss Crowninshield's grim, knotted face wavered just beyond the tears that were streaming from Sarah's eyes. The other shepherds, too, were flailing in the undertow.

"Dismissed!" cracked the voice. "Shepherds, you are dismissed!" The laughter died out. "You are to leave the stage. Go directly to the study hall."

The study hall was empty.

"Do you think we've actually been fired?" Sarah wondered aloud.

"I don't know," Elaine replied as she slipped into her chair. "Gosh, I hope my algebra book is here and not in homeroom. Ah, here it is!"

"Have you done those binomial expansions yet?" Hillary asked her.

"Two more to go."

Phoebe Buxton, a sophomore, got out her geometry gear and began inscribing arcs and circles through obtuse angles. Everyone seemed to have settled down nicely to study except Sarah. The great wave of hysteria had crested and broken, but some foam remained, stippling the surface and lapping at the low-tide mark. She fidgeted as the foam tickled her.

Elaine looked up from her algebra. "You're still laughing, aren't you, Benjamin."

"I can't help it. It was so funny."

"Try a binomial expansion. It's a sobering experience."

"I don't have my algebra book." The only book in Sarah's study-hall desk was her ancient history text. She opened it and tried to find something sobering. Something to counter her image of Lacey and Roger. Ah-ha! On page twenty-five in the chapter on Hebrews there was a photograph of the mummified body of Ramses II, the pharaoh thought to be the one who enslaved the Hebrews. Now, that's a very sobering picture. Mummies tend to be that way, Sarah guessed. He appeared gaunt, his lips pursed as if he had just sucked a lemon. There was a white halo around each eye in an otherwise dark face.

"Did the Egyptians have sunglasses back then?" Sarah asked, looking over at Phoebe.

"How should I know," Phoebe said, her face rather blank under its light cover of freckles. She had taken off her burnoose, and her short, dark, reddish hair was matted to her large head. She was a big girl and, hunched over her paper with protractor and compass, she appeared absolutely crammed into the small desk seat. Her cheesecloth shepherd robes bunched out the back slats of the seat. Hillary Daniels in her robes, on the other hand, looked like a small bag of laundry deposited on top of a desk. She was still wearing her burnoose and was now bent over her Latin translation. A faint whisper issued from the bag. *"Fanum est de cuius sanctitate omnes audivistis."*

Sarah said, "You think they had sunglasses, Daniels?"

"What?" Hillary looked up. "I'm trying to do this Latin translation. Does *cuius* mean 'temple' in Latin?"

"No!" said Sarah and Elaine.

" '*Cuius*' is a relative pronoun," Elaine offered.

"What's the sentence?" asked Sarah.

*"Fanum est de cuius sanctitate omnes audivistis."*

"It is a shrine about the sanctity of which you have all heard," Sarah translated quickly.

"See!" Elaine said. "Advanced Latin, here she comes."

"Forget it. Doesn't anybody know whether Egyptians had sunglasses?"

"Of course they did," Elaine said.

"What do you mean 'of course,' Bauer?"

"It's obvious. Remember what Miss Ulrich said. How they had those early papyrus rolls, the first books on surgery, math. They figured out that pi is 3.1416 sixteen hundred years before the birth of Christ. If they figured that out, you can bet sunglasses would have been a snap."

"If they were so smart," Hillary wondered aloud without a trace of sarcasm in her voice, "why didn't they make books instead of papyrus rolls?"

"Hmmm." Sarah sighed. "Well, in any case, I've never seen a picture of an Egyptian in sunglasses."

"Yes you have," Elaine said.

"Where?"

"Nasser, the president of Egypt, dummy. And that guy before him—the fat one—King Farouk."

"They don't count. I mean ancient Egypt."

"Oh."

The girls returned to their work. A few minutes later Sarah rapped on the desk excitedly with her pencil. "Hey! Hold everything, guys. An amazing discovery! Guess what?"

"What? Ancient Egyptians wore Bermuda shorts," Elaine supposed.

"Nope. Get this. Right here, page two twenty of our James Henry Breasted's *Ancient Times.*"

"Can you imagine having the last name Breasted?" Phoebe said. "How embarrassing!"

"He must have been a real boob! Ha-ha!" Elaine cackled. The other girls laughed.

"I'd change my name," said Hillary.

"Shut up and listen, you guys. 'The Hebrews were all originally men of the Arabian desert, wandering'——now get this—'with their flocks and herds and slowly drifting into their final home of Palestine.' "

"So what's the big deal?" Elaine asked.

"We were shepherds!"

"What do you mean, 'we'?" Phoebe said, looking up from her protractor.

"Well, okay, you're all Episcopalians, but I'm a Hebrew—a Jew, get it?"

"I'm not an Episcopalian," Hillary said hotly.

"What are you?" Sarah asked. "A Methodist?"

"Presbyterian."

"Well, it's basically all the same thing."

"It is not," Elaine replied.

"Okay. Okay. But you all agree that you're not Hebrew and I am? Right?"

"Right," they chorused.

"And you say that's the same as being Jewish?" asked Hillary.

"Right," Sarah confirmed. "Now listen to this: 'As the rough Hebrew shepherds looked across the highland of northern Palestine they beheld their kindred scattered over farstretching hilltops.' "

"Benjamin." Elaine Bauer closed her algebra book. "Why are you getting so excited about all this?"

46

"Well . . ." She thought to herself that she did indeed have reason to be excited. She thought she was going to learn something important about her ancestry. She thought that reading that Hebrews had been rough shepherds would . . . Her mind seemed to tumble into a void. Would what? Make being a shepherd better? worthier? more exciting? She had thought wrong. Just because a history book stated that Hebrews had been shepherds didn't make it any better. Ancient Hebrews probably found shepherding as boring as she did. Given the choice she would prefer to be a plastic surgeon or a concert pianist or a housewife rather than a shepherd—especially a stage shepherd. Anything was better than that.

Just at that moment Miss St. John poked her head into the room. "Girls," she said in her breathy voice.

Miss St. John was Miss Crowninshield's assistant. Her official title was vice principal. She had oatmeal-colored skin and wore her hair pulled back in a coil that lay at the nape of her neck like a knockwurst sausage. Miss St. John in her role as vice principal had remained in a state of almost total eclipse, a satellite to a larger celestial body—Crowninshield. She remained within that heavenly body's shadow with barely a cusp of her own presence visible to the rest of the world.

"Girls!" The four girls looked up. "Miss Crowninshield has sent me. She would like you to return to the stage if you can maintain appropriate behavior."

"I thought we were fired!" Elaine sighed. "All right! All right!"

Phoebe began putting away her compass and protractor and putting on her burnoose. Hillary folded her translation neatly and slid it into her Latin book. Elaine closed the parenthesis on her last binomial expansion, and Sarah slammed up Ramses in Breasted. Robes were adjusted, burnooses straightened.

"Okay," Phoebe said, unwedging herself from her seat and

47

stretching up to her full five-foot-eight. "As Robert Horton says on 'Wagon Train,' 'Head 'em up, move 'em out!' "

"Robert Horton doesn't say that," Hillary scoffed. "It's the other guy on the show, the old man, the wagon master."

"Not to mention that it's cattle, not sheep," Sarah added.

Miss Crowninshield did not acknowledge their return as they filed back onto the stage. She kept her eyes riveted on the Gospel of St. Luke. The shepherds reassembled themselves into their heap. Louanne had just finished playing the accompaniment for a solo.

"You know, Benjamin," Phoebe whispered very softly, "Louanne doesn't play nearly as well as Marla."

"Of course not. She's not a prodigy."

"Is your Aunt Hattie still in Marla's room?"

"Is she ever!" To Sarah it seemed as though she'd always been there.

Hattie had arrived within thirty-six hours of Marla's departure. She had been operated on the week before at Massachusetts General Hospital's Eye and Ear Clinic. She had not been planning to tell her sister until later, but Serge Vronsky had called and informed them. Shirley took the first plane to Boston. The call came the next evening. "Yeah. . . . Yeah. . . . Uh, sure." Alf had responded somberly, nodding into the telephone.

He turned to the girls. "Hattie's fine, but it was malignant. Quite contained; however, the left eye had to be removed."

"Oh no!" Marla gasped.

"You're kidding!" Sarah said.

"It's not so terrible. Believe me, girls, plenty of people have only one eye, and she's lucky. This kind of cancer is certainly not the worst kind, and the prognosis is very good. The surgery went well, and there is no chemotherapy to go through."

"But one eye!" Sarah said softly with wonder.

"Look, girls. It *is* sad, but there are many sadder situations, tragic situations. The disfigurements children are born with! If we're lucky we can try reconstruction. Hattie is not really disfigured. Hattie is not a child who must endure growing up and being taunted by peers. She will do fine." Alf put his arms around his daughters' shoulders. "Now. She's going to come here to recuperate. She'll come the day after you leave for college, Marla. We'll put her in your room." Alf talked on about arrangements: flights to and from Boston, Marla's going, Hattie and Shirley coming. "I'm going to have a phone line put in for her."

"A phone!" Sarah had been only half listening to the logistics surrounding Aunt Hattie's installation into their home. "How come Aunt Hattie rates a phone line? I've been living here for fourteen years and I've never gotten my own phone."

"Because you are not Hattie Silverman and Associates."

"I have plenty of associates."

"Look, Hattie's business requires that she be on the phone constantly. We can't have her tying up our line. If I get a call from the hospital saying a baby just had its ear torn off by a German shepherd—that happened today, incidentally—I can't wait for Hattie to finish one of her mother-confessor conversations with Vronsky over his most recent blini-and-chocolate-sundae binge."

So Hattie had arrived. After fourteen years of sharing the bathroom with Marla who had never complained about her messiness, who cheerfully wiped the hair out of the sink and recapped the toothpaste while humming a Bach prelude, she was sharing it with a one-eyed aunt who trilled hygenic aphorisms over running bathwater.

Sarah arrived home from school that November afternoon and

tapped on the bathroom door. "It's me, Aunt Hattie. Can I come in and get my pimple cream?"

"Of course, darling girl. I'm just taking a bath. Come in and keep me company. Tell me about that idiotic school you go to. It's such a charming anachronism."

Sarah walked into the steamy bathroom. Aunt Hattie, or The Hat, as Sarah sometimes referred to her, was steeping herself in the froth of a bubble bath. The bubbles mounded around her like cumulus clouds. She wore a bath bonnet and a black eye patch. Black, The Hat had declared, was the only color for an eye patch. Anything else was tacky, although the occupational therapist at the hospital had shown her a "rainbow selection" that could be coordinated with various outfits. Some were even studded with rhinestones. "Who do you think I am? Liberace?" Hattie had asked the therapist.

"No, black is the only appropriate color," Hattie had explained to Sarah and Shirley shortly after her arrival in Indianapolis. Certain things should come in only one color, one gender—one way, Hattie had said. "For example, we speak of painters, not paintresses. And I know for a fact," Hattie continued, "that Marianne Moore loathes being called a poetess. It's a diminution of an art." Hence, for Aunt Hattie, eye patches were black—always.

"So, what's an anachronism?" Sarah asked, rummaging through the medicine cabinet.

"You don't know that word? How will you ever get into Wellesley?"

Sarah grimaced and dabbed some flesh-colored cream on a spot on her chin.

"Aunt Hattie, I do wish that you would stop trying to arrange my life for me."

"I'm not arranging your life for you, Sarah. I merely suggested that an increased vocabulary would stead you well when it comes time for college applications. And by the way, dear heart, people pay substantial sums of money for me to arrange things for them."

Sarah would have paid substantial sums of money to *stop* Hattie from arranging things for her.

"An anachronism," Hattie continued, "is something that is out-of-date or, really, out of its proper historical time, to be more precise."

"Oh dear," Sarah said, examining her face more closely.

"What, more pimples?"

"No. I was just thinking about anachronisms and the fact that I've been put in an advanced Latin group."

"What does that have to do with anything?" Hattie said, as she languorously lifted a very thin arm from the bubbles and blew some froth from her fingertips.

Had it only been seven weeks ago that she had shared the bathroom with Marla? Marla never took baths; she showered. And when she showered she did her special exercises to develop the muscles and coordination required for the full arm strokes found in works like the Chopin études. The upper arm had to be strong, for it was the driving force behind the power and tone that were transmitted by the fingers. Sarah could picture Marla lean and wet, her shoulders and upper arms shapely as she flexed and swung them under the blast of the shower.

"I was just thinking," Sarah said, "how, rather than being advanced in an ancient civilization, I would prefer to be current in the present one."

Hattie fixed her good eye on Sarah. "What a charming, paradoxical creature you are, Sarah. You know, I'm not sure Wellesley really is the place for you. Maybe Bennington or Sarah Lawrence."

"Hmmm," said Sarah, leaning even closer to the mirror to pluck an eyebrow.

"Please, dear heart, don't let your brow hairs remain in the sink. It's most nauseating. You know I'm not one of those who says things like cleanliness is next to godliness. I think that is a terrible anthropomorphism of God. Look, I'm sharing the john with you. So let's just settle for cleanliness is next to Hattieness." Sarah's tweezers froze in midpluck while Hattie giggled raucously at her own joke.

# Chapter Six

$S$arah was standing near the gas station across the street from Stuart Hall, pumping quarters into a pay phone. It was recess and nervously she kept checking her watch. Her parents would have fits if they knew how many times a week she called Marla. A substantial portion of her allowance went to long-distance calls to Wellesley, Massachusetts. The phone had rung twice. Oh, she prayed that Marla was in. She knew that on Thursdays Marla did not have an early class, but her roommate did. Joy! There was the lovely click of the receiver being lifted.

"Hi, listen, before I get into the ablative absolute—guess what?"

"What?" Marla yawned.

"The Hat thinks she's God."

"What else is new?"

"No, I'm not kidding. It's awful. She's just beyond belief."

"You've always loved Aunt Hattie."

"Until I had to share a bathroom with her. She's also a klepto-maniac, by the way."

"C'mon, Sarah."

"No. She borrows my barrettes all the time without asking."

"Aunt Hattie doesn't wear barrettes. That's not her style."

"I know, but she likes those plastic tortoise-shell ones."

"Listen, Sarah." Sarah could tell that her sister was not fully awake. "You're going to have to handle this."

"That's easy for you to say from your nice ivy tower."

"I share a john with twenty other girls."

"Hmm. Well, I'd take twenty other girls over one Aunt Hattie. Have you met any Harvard guys yet?"

"A couple."

"Any dates with any of them?"

"One."

"Was he cute?"

"Not really. A girl on the first floor had a date with the Aga Khan."

"Who's that?"

"Isabelle Schaffer."

"No. I mean who's the Aga— Wait, I have to put in some more money." Sarah dug into her pocket and dropped in another thirty cents.

"Sarah, you don't know who the Aga Khan is?"

"It sounds sort of familiar."

"He happens to be the religious leader of all Moslems."

"Oh yeah, now I remember. Well, what's he doing at Harvard? Are there a lot of Moslems there?"

"No, Sarah, he's a student. Actually I think he's already graduated and was back for something else. She went out with him a few times last year."

"If I were the religious leader of all Moslems I wouldn't bother going to college. Sounds like a good job."

"Oh, Sarah!" Marla groaned. "Okay, what is it about the ablative absolute?"

"Look, Marla. I've got two sentences here. One is the ablative absolute and one is not. Now, why is *Incitatis equis hostes adoriebantur* the ablative absolute, but *Nuntium captum ad Caesarem adduxerunt* isn't?"

54

"Wait. Now, what are you trying to say in English? Spurring on their horses they attacked the enemy and what was the other one? *Nuntium captum ad Caesarem . . .*"

"This is the operator." The mechanical voice broke through the Latin.

"No! Wait a minute, operator." Sarah frantically dug into her pocket again and found some more change. "*Ad Caesarem adduxerunt.*"

muttering rules about participial phrases ·and ablative absolutes. Latin wasn't until fifth period. She had to keep all of this in her head through French and then lunch.

She was just putting her books in her locker when Elaine Bauer came up to her. "I've got a problem about the dance."

"Look," Sarah said. "I don't mean to cut you off but I can't talk right now. I have to study this ablative absolute stuff and keep it in my brain until the Latin quiz."

"It's not that hard, Benjamin."

"For me it is. I promise I'll listen to your problem about the dance during basketball practice."

How much of a problem could Bauer have? She at least had been invited to the Thanksgiving dance, the Turkey Trot, as it was unfortunately called. Sarah hadn't even been invited.

"*Bonjour, mes filles! Allons! Une dictée aujourd'hui.*" Madame spoke cheerfully as the girls settled themselves into their seats. "Let's get moooving," Madame continued in English, "so we can finish this *dictée* and have some fun. I brought some pictures to show today."

"Yea! Yea!" The girls shouted. Everyone loved Madame's pictures from her vacations in France.

"*Alors! La dictée.*" She never used anything from the French grammar for these exercises. In fact, Mme. Henri rarely referred to their textbooks at all. She taught primarily from her own experiences. Nothing that happened to Madame was too small or too ordinary for comment or celebration. She found a significance—often a romantic one—in the most mundane events. So the girls listened avidly as Madame began by telling them she could not sleep the other night. Finally, at two in the morning, she got up and fixed herself a little glass of schnapps—oooh, it was so cold! And she wrapped herself in her silk wrapper, and over that "because it was steel so cold girls I put on my fur coat and snuffler."

"Snuffler!" the girls cried. "You mean muffler!"

"Yes, muffler—the Irish mohair one. Anyway, I picked up a book I had not read in so long—Colette—and ooh la la. The words were so beautiful. So this morning I decided instead of the *dictée* I had planned, the one from that domb book *Civilisation Française,* that book we never use . . . Actually girls there is a nice *dictée* in there on the Pyrenees Mountains, but I thought how much more fun to give a *dictée* from Colette. So this is the book. It is called *Chéri and the Last of Chéri.* It is—oooh!" Madame clutched the book to her breast and rolled her eyes toward the ceiling. The large amber silk foulard at her neck set off her delicate face. *"Comment dit-on en anglais?* How does one explain this in English to you young silly girls? Well, it is about a woman who is not old, but not young. Oh, maybe forty-five or so."

"That's old!" said Helen Claflin.

"It's not that old, *chérie!* Anyway, she is in love with a young man of, say"—Madame looked carefully at the girl—"oh, say nineteen."

"Nineteen! That's sickening."

"Ugh!"

"That's finky!"

"He must be a jerk."

56

"It is not feenky and you should all know such jerks!" Madame protested. "It is beautiful. And now the part I shall read to you takes place in the woman's apartment. Lea is her name and the young man is there." Madame began to read. A look of sheer transport bathed her face.

"I have no idea what this means," Elaine whispered to Sarah.

*"Avez-vous une question, Elaine?"*

"I don't understand all these words."

*"Quels mots?"* Madame walked over to Elaine and looked down at her paper. "Oooh! *Il faut les comprendre.* I shall translate for you. It says he was capering nude." The girls became hysterical. *"Fermez les bouches*—shut up your mouths please," Madame ordered. *"Alors,* he was 'capering nude' in front of the sun-drenched rosy-pink curtains—'a graceful demon against a glowing furnace.' "

The ablative absolute went out the window, right out the sun-drenched rosy-curtained window. Sarah loved Madame's dictation. She was one of the few teachers in the school who seemed to have had a real life, real experiences. Sarah looked down at Madame's hand. A long finger, its joints swollen with arthritis, pointed to the words on Elaine's paper. The hand had age spots. The skin was so thin and dry that it seemed like tissue paper. Yet it was a hand that had held champagne glasses and felt rose-tinged light and touched lovers, too. Yes, Madame had lived.

# Chapter Seven

"**N**o. No. I agree," Sarah said on the phone that evening. "It's a problem, Elaine."

Shirley peered into the den where Sarah was talking and mouthed the word *dinner* and held up five fingers.

"Yes, well, it is sort of hard for me to relate to, seeing as I don't have a date for the dance. But I agree proctology is not an ideal profession. Yes, plastic surgery is better; but we can't exactly trade fathers for the evening."

"What!" Shirley exclaimed from the doorway. "What in the heck are you talking about?"

Sarah put her hand over the receiver. "I'll explain later, Mother. Please, let me finish."

Shirley crossed her eyes, scratched her head, and left.

"But if I were you," Sarah continued, "I wouldn't be getting so upset about it. I mean, realistically what do you think the chances are that he'll ask you all about your dad's profession? . . . Yeah. . . . Yeah, I know. Well, let me think on it. Maybe *Roget's Thesaurus* has something. . . . Okay, talk to you later."

Sarah hung up and went into the living room. Aunt Hattie was coiled in a wing chair, sipping a martini. She wore a black silk kimono with bright red poppies floating across it. On her feet were gold slippers, the toes of which curled up into dragon heads. She had offered to order Sarah some from Paris. Sarah looked at her now. She was wearing another one of Sarah's barrettes, a bright red one to match the poppies. She might have asked!

"What's up, toots?" Hattie inquired cheerfully as she stretched her feet toward the logs blazing in the fireplace and waggled the dragon heads. In addition to calling her toots and borrowing her barrettes without permission, one of the things that really got Sarah about her aunt was The Hat's fakey little youthful gestures. She was always trying to act like a teenager—wiggling her toes! Worse yet was the night she demonstrated the new dance called the Twist when Elaine and Hillary were over. Terminal embarrassment—a fifty-two-year-old, one-eyed aunt in her red silk "coolie trousers" and mandarin jacket doing the Twist.

"Elaine Bauer has a problem," Sarah replied.

"What's that?" her father asked. He was stirring a drink at a table that served as a small bar.

"Is there any other word or name or nice way of putting something—"

"You mean a euphemism?" Hattie offered.

"Yes, a euphemism."

"A euphemism for what?" her father asked, popping an olive into his mouth.

"For what a proctologist does?"

Alf choked and the olive blew straight out of his mouth and hit an English botanical print hanging on the wall. Alf started to laugh. "Why do you have to have this euphemism?" He took his handkerchief out of his back pocket and wiped his mouth.

"I don't. Elaine Bauer needs it."

"Oh, I understand. Norton is a proctologist."

"Yes, and she has to go to this Thanksgiving dance with this real cute guy. It's sort of a blind date, and she's scared that he's going to ask her what her father does."

"So?" Shirley had come into the room. "She'll just say her

59

dad's a proctologist and that'll be the end of it—no pun intended."
The adults chortled.

"Look," said Sarah. "You guys might think it's funny, but I am sure glad Daddy is a plastic surgeon and not a proctologist having to look up people's rear ends."

"Her date won't even know what a proctologist is," said Hattie.

Grown-ups were so dense. In measured tones Sarah began to spell it out for them. "That is just the problem. He won't know what it is, so he'll ask and then Elaine will have to explain. Now, how do you explain a profession like that? Dad, are there any other words that aren't quite so, so—oh, you know what I mean."

"Hah! We had some names for those guys in medical school, but I doubt . . ." He began to laugh again.

"You guys are terrible. You don't know what it's like. We're all social retards from going to an all-girls' school. Here Elaine is invited to her first formal dance. She's got all sorts of pressures. This guy is really cute. She just doesn't want to have to deal with this kind of issue. I swear it would almost be better to be an orphan than have a dad who's a proctologist."

"God forbid," Hattie and Alf chorused.

"Bite your tongue!" Shirley said.

"Sorry, Dad."

"Don't apologize to me. Apologize to Norton Bauer. Why do you think I decided on plastic surgery? I didn't want to inflict such pain on an adolescent daughter or, worse yet, be murdered by her." He chuckled merrily. "Okay, I've got it. She can say that her father deals with the lower intestine . . . sort of a lower-tract man."

"Very lower, I'd say," Hattie added.

"Well, it all more or less hooks up."

"That sounds good," Sarah said. "I'm going to call Elaine."

"First dinner, please," Shirley said. "If you can eat after this discussion."

"What dance is this?" Hattie asked. She ate European style, keeping her fork in her left hand, and was about six inches away from putting a piece of chicken in her mouth.

"Turkey Trot," Sarah answered.

Hattie's hand froze in its ascent. "Turkey Trot?" she articulated carefully. "You must be joking."

"Nope, and I'm not invited."

"It's a blessing," said Hattie as she bit into her chicken and reached for her glass of water.

"That's your perspective," Sarah answered.

Hattie looked over the rim of the glass. "You know, dear heart, I think only in Indiana would they call a dance a Turkey Trot."

Shirley leaned toward her sister. "Well, it's one of our quaint midwestern customs. We can't all go to the April in Paris Ball in New York." Shirley gave Alf a veiled dark look. Sarah knew that her mom got irritated with The Hat, too.

"Now, don't get huffy, Shirl," Hattie said. "I was only trying to solace Sarah." She turned back to her niece. "You think these things are so important," she intoned. "These little adolescent problems loom so much larger than they actually are or need be."

Golly, Hattie could be aggravating, Sarah thought. Granted, not going to the Turkey Trot was preferable to having cancer and losing an eye.

"You know," Hattie continued, "you will look back on this someday and it will be such a little . . . little . . . " She searched for a word.

"Zit," said Sarah.

"Yes. A zit on the mountain of life, or I should say face of life.

Speaking of your complexion, Sarah"——Hattie rolled on without missing a beat——"the next time you come to New York I'm going to treat you to a marvelous thing."

"What?" said Sarah, glowering. Why, oh why had she ever said the word *zit*?

"I am going to make an appointment for you with my marvelous Hungarian face lady. She will clear up all that stuff on you in no time." Hattie waved her thin hand in the direction of Sarah's face in a gesture that was designed to be executed with a wand. Sarah was seething. She detested Hattie's infinite volume of beauty tips. Along with those tips Hattie had an entire directory of body and beauty people who kept her in shape. She had a very proprietary attitude about people in general, so in addition to "my artists," it was always "my face lady," "my hair man," "my exercise woman." It came from being a manager, Sarah guessed.

"I don't want to go to your face lady."

"Oh, you should, darling. She's wonderful. I don't have overactive oil glands like you do—note the euphemism."

What was Sarah supposed to do, thank Aunt Hattie for not saying she had a zitty complexion?

"But at my age it's quite the reverse. Bodily fluids drying up. I'm virtually a Mojave Desert, skinwise."

"What about Death Valley," Sarah whispered. Her mother shot her a terrible look. Hattie merely continued talking.

"If it weren't for my Anya I'd be parched, cracked, and eroded." She sighed as she imagined the geological upheavals she had skirted thanks to "her Anya."

"What a pity," Sarah muttered softly.

"Sarah!" Shirley said. "Aunt Hattie is only trying to be helpful. I think it would be fun to have a facial. So luxurious."

"Yes, dear heart, we just don't want you to go directly from acne to wrinkles."

Alf made a face. "Sarah's just fine. So she's got a couple of spots. I would hardly call two spots an acne problem."

"Thanks," murmured Sarah.

"I'd also like to get Sarah to my Jerry."

Did this woman ever quit? "Who is 'my Jerry'?" Sarah asked stonily.

"He's a magician with hair. He'd get that hair off your forehead, which is probably causing your spots." .

Sarah's face tightened. She had never been so angry. "I don't need a magician. I need my barrette. Why don't you give me back my barrette, which you took without asking?"

"My, my! Aren't we all cranky tonight. Tell me, Sarah, are you accusing me of stealing?"

Shirley and Alf looked at each other in a panic. How had this feisty exchange escalated so fast?

"No, just borrowing without asking."

"Sarah!" Shirley exclaimed.

"Well, Marla and I always asked. We were very careful about that kind of stuff. We had kind of a set of laws, a code that applied to borrowing clothes and makeup. Aunt Hattie also used some of my bath cologne."

"Sarah! Cut it out!" Alf barked. "Or leave the table."

"I would never use your bath cologne, Sarah dear. It has a revolting, cloying smell. I wouldn't even call it a fragrance. And while we are on codes, how about applying Hammurabi's to the bathroom? An eye for an eye!" With that Hattie tore the red barrette from her hair, flung it to the table and stormed out of the room in a swirl of black silk and trembling red poppies.

"How could you, Sarah?" Shirley jumped up. Her face was flushed with anger.

"Me?" Sarah exclaimed. "How could *I*?" She burst into tears as Shirley rushed out of the dining room.

Alf stared at his plate. Sarah sniffled noisily. She slid her eyes toward her father. He just stared into his plate. Was he angry with her or what? This silence was awful. She sniffled louder and coughed a little. She began in a small voice. "She's so difficult, Dad." He fiddled silently with a crust of bread on his plate. "You just don't understand. She's so difficult."

Alf raised his head slowly. "You don't have to tell me how difficult Hattie is, Sarah. I have known her for thirty years. She can be selfish, pigheaded, arrogant, a baby. You name it. Yet for all those negatives there are positives, and that is what makes Hattie work. And now I am going to give you a lesson in family physics: Opposites attract. We are all as a family a bunch of positive and negative charges and therefore we all hang together. This is the nuclear family!" He stood up. His eyes bored into Sarah. "Hattie is part of this family. Do you understand? And you in your insensitivity and rudeness have thrown in an extra negative charge: You have upset the balance—the bonding. Now go in there and neutralize the situation this minute, Sarah Benjamin!"

Sarah immediately got up. She tried to keep her mind on what her dad had said—or perhaps what he had not said. Sarah had never taken physics, but it was clear to her that he had not said that she should apologize. He had not said what she had expected: that Hattie needed them because they were the only family Hattie had. No, he had turned it all around, in the name of science, and said that the nucleus of the atom would fly apart unless she . . . She didn't understand it, but she quickened her step to the back of the house. Her mother stood grim-faced outside Hattie's door. "She's locked it," Shirley said coldly. "Sarah! How could you?"

"Don't say anything more, Mom. I'm sorry. I really am. Let me talk to her."

"All right." Shirley turned and started toward the dining room.

Sarah knocked softly on the door. "Aunt Hattie? Hattie?" There was no answer. She quickly walked to the bathroom that connected their bedrooms. The door leading to Hattie's room was locked, but the keyhole was a large, old-fashioned one. Sarah got down on her knees and peered through the hole. Hattie was sitting quite erect on the edge of Marla's bed, twirling the bathroom key. A pool of light from the Mozart lamp illuminated her. Sarah was stunned to see that she was wearing a small fur hat. It was her new mink toque. Panic gripped Sarah. Was she going to leave? Had Sarah driven Aunt Hattie right out of the house? Sarah suddenly had a vivid picture of an atom. From its very center where the nucleus nestled, a fur-crowned creature came jetting out. Sarah pressed her face closer to the keyhole. She could see a bright tear coming out of Hattie's one eye. This was worse—worse than the flying mink-topped nuclear particle. She, Sarah Benjamin, had drawn this single silvery tear that was now making its wet course down Hattie's high cheekbones.

"Hattie!" Sarah whispered desperately. "You're crying!"

Hattie turned slowly toward the bathroom door and bent her head toward the keyhole. Her dark, straight, gray-streaked hair swung slightly forward under the mink. Her angular face seemed to contract as she focused on the keyhole. It was such a tiny, delicate face, Sarah thought. Why did part of it have to be missing?

"Yes, I am crying," Hattie said in a toneless voice. "You will note that I can still cry, even if I have only one set of tear ducts."

"Oh! Oh, Aunt Hattie! I am so sorry. I really am. Please, Aunt Hattie, forgive me." Sarah crumpled to the bathroom floor. She did not hear Hattie approaching, but the door suddenly swung open. She looked up from the tile floor and was eye to eye with the little dragon-headed slippers.

"Well . . ." The left little dragon tapped on the tile floor. "Just because I can cry only from one eye doesn't mean I can't appreciate two eyes crying." The kimono seemed to collapse, engulfing Sarah in a cloud of black silk. "Now, now, Sarah!" Hattie's thin arms wrapped around Sarah's shoulders. Her spiky fingernails ran gently through Sarah's hair. "You see, it's just like we're sisters—sharing a bathroom, arguing about things. It's so much fun to be a sister for a change instead of a manager."

It was nothing like having a sister! And as far as Sarah could tell, she was still trying to manage everything. But how could Sarah say this when here she was curling her thin, black-silked body around Sarah—and the truth was that despite all the hard angles and the protruding bones, it felt okay. She looked up. "Why are you wearing your new mink hat?"

"Just trying it on for Chicago."

"Chicago?" Sarah said blankly. "Oh yeah, Vronsky's performance."

"Yes, dear heart, I have to start being a manager again sometime. *Sleeping Beauty,* a week from this Friday."

"The night of the Turkey Trot," Sarah said dully.

"Oh, forget the damn Turkey Trot. Come to Chicago with us and see *Sleeping Beauty.* Come on. Your mother's coming. I bet if you came your dad would try to switch his schedule and come, too."

"Hmm."

"Come on now. It'll be so much fun. We'll all stay at the Drake. You haven't seen Serge dance in a long time."

"Last time I saw him in *Sleeping Beauty,* I was nine."

"Well, don't expect what you saw at nine, but he's in relatively good shape and we have a very light ballerina for the princess. You know the last act after the marriage has all those lifts. We're not going to have him throw his back out like he did in Los Angeles last year with that blimp."

# Chapter Eight

The ballerina was no blimp.

"Good Lord!" Alf whispered just after Princess Aurora had finished her dance with the four princes in the second scene of Act I. "She looks like she just got out of a concentration camp."

"*Sssh!*" Shirley jabbed her husband with her elbow.

From their fifth-row center seats, Sarah could indeed count Aurora's ribs through the bodice of her pink and silver costume. She did not know what shape Vronsky was in, for he had not yet made his entrance, but Sarah felt that she herself could have lifted this bag-of-bones Princess and walked to the shores of Lake Michigan and back with her. The ballerina, despite her wraithlike appearance, was an all-right dancer. This was of course part of Hattie's responsibility as a manager: to find adequate, not brilliant, dancers to serve as foils to the waning glow of Serge's virtuosity. His days with the great primas were over. Now he needed good, serviceable ballerinas who were not too heavy.

In another five minutes scene 2 was over. The Princess, having pricked her finger on the Evil Fairy's spindle, had conked out. The rest of the court joined immediately in the timeless slumber. Then, in what Sarah felt was the most spectacular part of the ballet, the Lilac Fairy appeared. She waved her wand and began what Sarah called the "vegetable variation." Vines crept up, cobwebs descended, brambles ensnared, until the palace and all the sleeping figures were locked in an impenetrable labyrinth. The scenery engineering was extraordinary.

It was Hattie's sacred obligation to the audience as well as to Serge to present him as well as could possibly be "managed" whether he was five pounds too heavy or not. Vronsky's contract included certain set design and lighting specifications. Hattie knew the most capable, artistic lighting technicians and insisted that only those men and women be hired. All of this detail served to enhance her artist.

Act II, scene 2. Years had passed. A blast of English hunting horns announced the Prince's hunting party. Vronsky strode in at its head wearing a jaunty cap and boots. There was a warm roar from the audience.

"He looks okay," Shirley whispered. Sarah didn't know how her mother could tell yet. All he had done so far was walk, or rather stride, across the stage. There were casks of wine, lots of grapes, lots of frolicking around, toots on hunting horns—your basic guy-in-tights-in-the-woods scene, Sarah thought.

"That's the Prince's henchman, right?" she whispered to her mother. "The guy in the cloak?"

"Not his henchman, Sarah! His tutor."

The hunting party was now engaged in a game of blindman's buff. Everyone was playing except the Prince. Vronsky did this standing-still routine very well, Sarah thought. While everyone else was pushing each other about, the Prince, standing apart, became perfectly still as if attuned to something else. Vronsky's body in the stillness of its pose was quite eloquent. Suddenly behind the gauzy scrims, or curtains, there was a soft glow as a lake appeared. On the lake was a mother-of-pearl boat sailed by the Lilac Fairy. The pas de deux seemed shorter than Sarah remembered. She supposed it had been scaled down. It lasted about fifteen seconds and consisted of some walking mixed with head nodding. No big jump, nothing too athletic.

"Very nice," whispered Shirley. But Sarah sensed more relief than awe in her voice. Then came the clouds. Hattie's favorite "cloud man," a lighting technician named Max, was responsible: Max Knight, who specialized in cloud effects and, in Hattie's words, next to the Big Cloud Man (she would point to the sky), was the best in the business.

The clouds were superb. They rolled back into a fog; then a dense haze descended, which peeled back and lifted, leaving only a gossamer mist. Behind the mist slept Princess Aurora on her golden couch. The Prince, of course, was smitten. Although "smatten," Sarah thought, might be a better word, as Vronsky fell to his knees in a kind of *plop* of adoration. She figured, however, that nobody behind the tenth row could hear the *plop*.

Vronsky rose as if in a trance and began his doleful dance of yearning. The Princess had left the chaise wrapped in a cobwebby kind of dress. Vronsky danced an ardent and, for him, strenuous variation as he followed her through layers of mist, clouds, cobwebs, and vines. There was a great deal of walking, posing, some running, no leaps. Still, the audience was as entranced with their own vision of Serge Vronsky, the great Russian dancer, as the Prince was with his Princess Aurora. Despite the years, despite the weight, despite the injuries, he still possessed a magical quality that both projected and protected a vision. The muscle, the sinew, the breath of lung perhaps had faded and diminished, yet the vision itself endured. A gossamer, stealthy creation still cast its spell.

The grand pas de deux in the last act was nothing like what Sarah remembered. There were lifts, but not as many as Sarah had expected, and only two or three catlike springs in the air. Each time he did one Sarah felt her mother tense up beside her.

At last it was over. It seemed to Sarah that Vronsky's curtain calls were as elaborate as his dancing. The balletomanes, the most ardent of ballet fans, crowded down the aisles and bombarded him with flowers, both real and paper. With baroque bows and sweeps he picked several up and presented them to Aurora, and he even rakishly tucked one blossom behind his ear, to the near-hysteria of his following.

Backstage, Hattie stood by Vronsky's dressing room in her mink bombardier jacket and matching toque, stolid as a Roman centurion. Nobody got past Hattie who was not supposed to. For twenty-five years she had protected her artists from the overexuberance of fans. And despite her thinness, her diminutive proportions, there was nothing frail in her appearance as she stood in the doorway receiving compliments, gifts, and messages for her artist. These backstage performances were every bit as important as those onstage. There was ritual. There was pageantry, and magic and power. At a certain moment the door to the dressing room was opened just a crack to yield glimpses of Vronsky wrapped in a sumptuous velvet robe the color of rubies. He could be seen reclining against a small mountain of heavily brocaded pillows. An oriental rug covered the dressing-room floor. A silver stand held a bottle of champagne.

"Of course, darling. I shall be sure to tell him," Hattie was saying to one wan-looking girl. "Christina! More of your lovely fabric flowers!" A rather chunky young woman with glasses had just presented Hattie with a spectacular bouquet of flowers sewn from glazed chintz. "You know, dear, those tapestry ones you did years ago for Giselle he still has in his Paris apartment, and the Swan Lake feather water lilies I believe he has in New York or Connecticut. Oh, marvelous! Christina! Here darling, here's a pass for rehearsal tomorrow. No you can't come in now. He's quite exhausted."

Sarah and her parents approached. As Shirley came up to the

door Hattie shoved a golden box into her hands. "They're Godiva chocolates. You can have them and for God's sake don't let him see them. Keep them under your coat. He'd go through the whole box tonight." Shirley slid the box under the coat she was carrying over her arm. Hattie waved the three of them into the dressing room. Sarah felt so important. It was exciting, there was no denying it. This did beat the Turkey Trot.

The dressing room, like Vronsky's apartments, was a glittering ornamented environment, a little construction of enchantment, of transport. He always kept the lights low after performances. Serge jumped up from the cushions. "Alf! Shirley! Saar-ah! My leetle *Saaar*-ah! You have grown. I vould not bel*eeeve* it!" He smacked his forehead with the heel of his palm, turned in profile, and gazed at the ceiling. He bowed deeply, grabbed Sarah's and her mother's hands to kiss each of them, stepped back still holding their hands, looked at them with relish, pranced forward to kiss their cheeks European-style, once on each side, then let go and leaped toward Alf and engulfed him in a huge hug. His robe, open at the top, revealed a smooth, tanned, hairless chest. Sarah thought of her own dad's thick mat of black and gray hair ending at a mild paunch of a stomach. Vronsky was squeezing her father so hard and crushing Alf's face against his shoulder that Alf's nose was squooshed sideways against his own cheek. When Vronsky finally released him Alf seemed slightly winded, his tie was askew, and he had a streak of makeup on his forehead.

"Champagne! Champagne!" Vronsky called. "Michael!" A young man came forward with a tray. "Ah, this is Michael, my valet. Michael, these are the Benjamins—Shirley, Alfred and darling Saar-ah. Saar-ah can have some champagne?" Vronsky asked, turning to Shirley and Alf.

"Sure, why not?" Alf said.

Michael handed Sarah a glass of champagne. Against one wall was a huge platter of fruit and another with cold cuts on a long table. "Help yourself," Michael said to Sarah. Then he whispered, "It's all low cal"—he rolled his eyes toward the ceiling—"so it might not interest you that much."

Sarah went over with her glass and took a small bunch of grapes. She noticed a woman sitting in a chair just by the dressing table. She was stunning. She had a shining helmet of blonde hair pulled back in a twist. Around her neck she wore a choker of diamonds, and she was dressed in a black velvet suit that clung to her body. She did not smile. Her face was expressionless, and the large, luminous gray eyes seemed to stare right through Sarah. Sarah stared right back. Why not? That was what this whole thing was all about—looking at pretty people, resplendent objects.

Hattie now shut the door and, whirling across the room, began functioning as the official hostess. "Paul, have you met my sister, Shirley? Paul's the *Trib*'s dance critic. Retired now. Isn't it nice just to come and enjoy and not have to run back to your typewriter?" Hattie went on with the introductions. Besides the retired dance critic, there was Morris, a documentary filmmaker; Henri, Vronsky's masseur; then Claire, a publicist; Kup, a columnist; and finally there was Helaine, the blonde in the black velvet suit. "Helaine." Hattie gave a brittle smile. (Sarah could see how unattractively the skin creased and pulled around Hattie's eye patch.) "I don't believe you've met my sister and brother-in-law from Indianapolis, Shirley and Alf Benjamin." She paused and then, looking at Alf with a twinkle in her single eye, said, "He is a man that every beautiful woman wants to meet after—how should I put it—a certain age."

"Oh," said Helaine coolly.

Shirley pinched Hattie's shoulder playfully. "Honestly, Hattie, you're too much!"

"He's a plastic surgeon!" Vronsky exclaimed, and then roared with laughter.

"Oh you're kidding!" Michael said, looking up from the tray of champagne glasses. "My aunt just had a nose job and, I don't know, I think she looked better before."

Oh no, Sarah thought. If they got onto plastic surgery and everybody started asking her dad questions— But Hattie deftly retrieved the situation and began with a few quick comments to direct the conversation toward the performance: The grand pas de deux had been so splendid and the variation in Act II exquisite.

Sarah sank back in a chair and watched and listened. Vronsky was of course the center of attention. He stretched languorously on his pillows. He talked of his Tartar village. He recalled a near disaster years ago when some scenery had fallen during the first act of *Swan Lake,* the professionalism of Maria Tallchief as she whispered orders in his ear and then pirouetted across the stage to the other swans to tell them exactly where to move. He talked of his tailor in Paris, his art dealer in New York, his gardener in Connecticut. He talked about swimming off the coast of Turkey, and the awful dressing rooms at the Paris Opera House. He talked about the Tolstoy short story "The Cossacks" that he planned to choreograph. He talked and talked and talked.

Sarah looked on and sometimes watched Helaine watching Vronsky. The woman was so still and golden and silent. But there was something utterly treacherous about her, and when Sarah saw her lightly finger her diamond choker she felt chills run down her own spine. Still, it was all wonderfully exciting and mysterious.

They did not get to bed until nearly two in the morning. Following the dressing-room celebration, they had gone to the Cape Cod Room, a restaurant in their hotel. Much to Hattie's horror, Serge downed a bowl of lobster bisque. "Serge, no!" Hattie exclaimed as the waiter set down the bowl. Pats of butter floated like islands on the thick soup.

"Darling, I cannot come here without ordering this. I adore it."

"Lobster's an aphrodisiac," Helaine said in a low, throaty voice.

"An aphro-what?" Sarah asked, looking up from her Coke.

"Butter is not," said Hattie testily.

"What's an aphrodisiac, Mom?" Sarah whispered.

"You know—food thought to enhance the power of love. Helps make someone a better lover."

Sarah looked at Helaine. The woman had all the warmth of an icicle in a January blizzard. She should take a long bath in hot lobster soup and apply butter liberally.

"What's with Helaine?" Sarah asked just before Hattie turned off the bedside light in the room they were sharing. Although Hattie did not usually wear her eyepatch to bed, she did tonight in deference to Sarah. She took care always to warn Sarah: "Wait just a minute, I'm patchless," she would say.

Hattie turned onto her side and propped herself up on one elbow. The shoestring strap of her nightgown slipped off one shoulder. Her shoulders and collarbone jutted out with all the cragginess of an alpine range; her face was smeared with cream; she had monster hair rollers pinned to the top of her head. She looked amazingly similar to a gigantic mutant insect in one of those science fiction horror movies. But she smiled a tender, sad smile and her one good eye brimmed with a kind of dolorous wisdom. "What's with Helaine?" She repeated the question. "She's rich. She's bored. And she's a failed dancer. That's what's with her and it makes her treacherous as hell!" Hattie turned off the light and pulled the covers up to her chin.

So Sarah had been right—treacherous. The Hat has used the very same word she had thought of earlier herself. "So why does Vronsky hang around with her?" she asked through the dark.

"He only occasionally hangs around with her."

"But why?"

Hattie sighed. "Did you notice how blank her face was? Her eyes?"

Sarah recalled the clear, pale eyes, like shallow reflecting pools. "Yes."

"Well, Serge . . ." Hattie paused. "Serge needs mirrors—looking glasses—and that is Helaine's function. She reflects his own light. I can't do that. I have to manage him. I cannot simply be a glazed surface with wonderful reflecting capabilities."

"Does Serge have other mirrors?"

"A few. There is a vicomtesse in Paris and someone in Texas."

"Are they all so treacherous?"

"Not quite."

"But does it worry you? I mean, if they are treacherous, couldn't they hurt Serge?"

Hattie laughed softly. "No, no, dear. Serge is vain, but he is very smart." She sighed. "God forbid I should get an artist who is vain and dumb. What do I mean! I've already had one."

"Who?" Sarah asked.

"Oh, that was years ago, when I was first getting started in the business. It nearly made me give up and become a kindergarten teacher."

"You! A kindergarten teacher!" Sarah laughed. "Fat chance."

"Nonsense! I would have given all the little tykes violins, hired Suzuki or one of his disciples—that was long before it was so popular over here," she said, referring to the Japanese master violin teacher's method. "I would have had them all booked in Carnegie Hall by Christmas."

"Mmm." Sarah sighed sleepily. But sleepy as she was, her mind was keen to thoughts of women. There were so many kinds—looking-glass women with treachery in their souls; managing women, like The Hat; women women, like her mother; and near women who were prodigies, like Marla. She pictured them in all their hues and variations and tones; like a rainbow they arced across the sky. And she pictured herself—earthbound and pale, standing in her saddle shoes, looking up until her neck ached, wondering about a future that was quite conditional.

# Chapter Nine

It was the last week in January. Sarah lay awake in the early morning wishing that she could stay under her warm quilts all day. The frosted windowpanes were like lace doilies. It was bitter cold outside, a fracturing kind of cold that seemed to make the air very brittle. Trees creaked and sunlight shattered across snowy lawns. But inside there were the warm sounds of early morning.

Both Shirley and Hattie had finished their respective shower and bath. Each stood naked now in her own bathroom, and Sarah could just hear the postbathing procedures, namely the application of after-bath tonics and colognes. How different the fleshly resonances were. The variation in tone was amazing, Sarah thought. Her mother was a comfortably cushioned size ten, and the cologne went on with nice, solid thwacking sounds as pink flesh with a decent subcutaneous layer was slapped with fragrant applications of Jean Naté After Bath Splash. Hattie's body, however, produced an entirely different tone. Little thwicky-thwicky sounds emanated from the bathroom with its half-open door on Sarah's side as Hattie applied an expensive floral fragrance to her bone-thin body. Sarah decided it actually sounded like mice tap dancing on tile.

Christmas vacation had been too short. Marla had come. She gave one recital—some Debussy. She and Sarah went to a lot of foreign films, and Marla, on Sarah's insistence, succumbed to one Western. They flew to Detroit with The Hat to see Vronsky in another performance of *Sleeping Beauty,* or The Big Sleep, as Marla called it; they got to shake hands with Henry Ford. They came back

77

to Indianapolis. Marla left. The Hat stayed. Hattie had midwestern and western engagements for Vronsky and a new Rumanian violinist she was managing. The poor Rumanian creature had arrived a year early from Bucharest. It could not be said that she had defected, although in truth she had. That particular verb was reserved for artists of greater stature—such as Vronsky in his celebrated grand jeté to freedom in London several years earlier. The violinist had just "arrived early."

With all this "western" work Hattie had decided to continue to sublet her New York apartment, at least until summer. She was feeling much stronger now, so she did a fair amount of traveling with her artists. When she was out of town managing Vronsky and the Rumanian and a string quartet group she had "discovered" in Bloomington at Indiana University Music School, life was great. But when she was not managing them she was managing Sarah. She had stopped taking Sarah's barrettes, but she had not stopped making suggestions about how Sarah should wear her hair. One evening, just to shut her up, Sarah let her fiddle with it. Sarah had very curly hair, which she hated. She was always trying to straighten it out with big rollers, hair sprays, various dekinking lotions, even an electric iron. She used the iron literally to press it into submission and straightness. Hattie's idea was that Sarah should not "restrain" her hair, but instead "let it express its natural buoyancy, dear heart."

"It's not a lifeboat. It's my hair!"

"It's so thick and luxuriant, Sarah dear." The long, curved, lacquered fingernails raked through it. Sarah closed her eyes and tried to banish fantasies of murder. If there was one thing she could not stand it was people messing with, commenting on, rendering advice about her hair. It was hers, after all. It was about the only thing she owned, could attempt to have control over. At fourteen everything else in her life was arranged and directed by other people.

She bossed her hair. Now here was The Hat—born to manage, the congenital boss, management in the chromosomes—attempting a takeover.

"Your face has such lovely contours, Sarah, and yet they are not revealed when you slick all that hair down and let it hang around your cheeks. Really, Sarah, you look so doleful—like one of those nuns who takes vows of silence. That's it! Locked behind a wimple of silence. Repressed!"

"I'm not a nun!" yelled Sarah. "I haven't taken any vows of silence, so I'm telling you to shut up!"

But The Hat would not shut up. The subject came up with startling regularity. Finally, Sarah succumbed to what Hattie called her "tonsorial ministrations" in hopes that Hattie would get it out of her system. The agreement was that Hattie could fix Sarah's hair any whichway, as long as she didn't cut it. If Sarah liked it she would keep it that way. If not, Sarah would wear it the way she wanted and no more would be said ever again about Sarah's hair. Fair enough. So the session began.

"I know you and all your friends want to look like Jackie Kennedy with that nice bouffant, pouffy look. Well, we can't all look like her."

"So what else is new?" Sarah muttered grimly as she sat in front of the mirror and The Hat went to town teasing and fluffing out her hair in all directions.

"I was saying to Lieba the other night before her concert at Bowling Green State College . . ."

*"I don't want to look like Lieba!* She is the creepiest-looking thing that ever crawled out from under the iron curtain."

"Sarah, you're so parochial! 'Under the iron curtain'—as if she's some sort of rodent. Next thing you're going to be doing is calling her a Commie creep."

"I am not. She's not a Commie anymore. She's just a creep. That frizzled hair! She looks just like Mozart."

"Listen, if you could have heard her the other night playing the Dvořák concerto it wouldn't have mattered if she were bald."

"Yes it would—ouch!"

"Just a tangle."

"If she were bald you would have made her get a wig or a transplant."

"You know, Serge is thinning considerably on top," Hattie said, going to work with her rat-tailed comb.

"Well, that's about the only place."

"Ha-ha! Very funny. No, seriously, I think he might want to consider a transplant."

"No he wouldn't."

"Why not?"

"It's one of the goriest operations Dad does, if you ask me. I just saw some pictures that he's putting in an article he's writing. It's almost as sickening as a face-lift."

"Well, Serge wouldn't have to watch."

"How bald is he?"

"What do you mean, how bald?"

"Well, fifty percent, twenty-five percent?"

"Heavens, no. You've seen him. It's a spot about the size of a large half-dollar."

"Hey, Dad!" Sarah called out across the hall to her parents' bedroom, where her dad was reading. "How many plugs do you need for a hair transplant the size of a large half-dollar?"

"Not very many," he called back. "Fifty or so, tops."

"Your own plugs are looking adorable," Hattie cooed. "Now for this little bow."

Sarah looked at herself. She had bubbles of curls framing her face and rippling off her brow. Hattie had just put in the bow.

"You're right. I don't look anything like Jackie Kennedy. I look like something out of the *Nutcracker Suite*."

"So what's wrong with that?" Hattie said, patting her creation.

"Nothing except I hate it. Now will you kindly shut up about my hair. Mother!" Sarah screamed. "Plug in the iron!"

In the future, Hattie would say nothing more about Sarah's hair. Not in words, at least. She would just roll her eyes on occasion, shoot knowing looks at Shirley, and never fail to comment on everybody else's hairstyle.

The styling experiment had been last night. Now on this cold January morning, as Sarah lay in bed she wondered if she was developing a strong moral character. What other reason could there be for all this misery? Lately she had been thinking about it a lot. She had read that Prince Charles was being sent to a very strict and rigorous school in Scotland where students had to rise at six in the morning, take freezing-cold showers, and run a mile before breakfast. On the moral development chart, she wondered how that compared to being yakked at by The Hat. About equal, she would guess. Surely there were better ways. Vestal virgins, selected for the supreme honor of serving in the temple of Vesta and tending the sacred fire in ancient Rome, had great moral fiber—and if they didn't they were entombed alive. In Sarah's ancient-history course they had finally gotten out of the Fertile Crescent and Mesopotamia and were creeping up on the Western world. They had more or less arrived at Greece and Rome. Sarah loved reading historical novels about it all. She had a penchant for the ones about slave girls in love with Roman aristocrats or aristocratic girls in love with slave boys. Sarah would have loved to live back in those days, if only they hadn't spoken Latin.

But what had she done to deserve entombment with Aunt Hattie?

"Sarah," said Hattie, coming into her bedroom wrapped in a

terry-cloth towel that morning, "aren't you up yet? It's late."

"Isn't it obvious that I'm not up yet?" She nestled down farther under her covers.

"Come on, you must get up."

"It's too cold."

"Nonsense! Did you read that piece in the paper about Prince Charles at Gordunstoun? Up at six, cold showers, cross-country runs before breakfast. Come on, toots, toughen up!"

Sarah yawned. "See my clothes over there?" She pointed to a chair over which her navy blue school uniform, underwear, and blouse were draped.

"Yes."

"Would you please hand them to me."

"Why?" Hattie paused. "Don't tell me, Sarah Benjamin, that you're going to get dressed in bed?"

"You bet."

"No."

"I always do in subzero weather."

"Sarah, your sloth knows no bounds."

"Hmmm," Sarah said.

"You mean I can't shame you into getting out of bed?"

"No. Just hand over the clothes, please."

Hattie did, and Sarah proceeded to get dressed under the covers.

"Sarah, what I came in here to talk to you about was not your sloth."

"Oh, boo-hoo," Sarah sobbed.

"Well, perhaps it relates. You see, I had a marvelous decorating idea for the bathroom."

"Whoopee!" said Sarah, buttoning her blouse while lying flat on her back.

"Yes, dear heart. You know the bathroom is awfully cute, especially when it doesn't have your hair plastered to various surfaces. I mean that marble sink and those old-fashioned fixtures and the brass wall hooks and all the other details."

"Yes?"

"Well, I was thinking about a new coat of paint and a few plants."

"Who needs plants in a bathroom?"

"Well, I think a touch of greenery—"

"I think it's dumb. Look, Aunt Hattie, we don't go in there to farm. Is this one of your ideas from that fancy New York store you're always talking about—Blooming Valley's?"

"Bloomingdale's, you mean. No, dear heart." The eye squinted and contracted into a little black slash. "I don't get ideas from Bloomingdale's. If anything, they get them from me." She was referring, of course, to the time all the windows on Lexington Avenue were filled with stunning photo murals of Serge Vronsky dancing *Les Sylphides*. "I am not one of those little brides coming in for her wicker and chintz chachkas."

"What are chachkas?" Sarah asked.

"Are you Jewish or what?"

"Of course I am. But you're a New York Jew and I'm a Hoosier Jew. What are chachkas?"

"Yiddish for *trinkets*—unnecessary stuff. Anyway, I thought we might just do the walls of the bathroom in a nice shade of crème de cacao."

"Kram de what? Would you quit speaking Yiddish."

*"Oy vey!"* Hattie rolled her eye toward the ceiling. "Crème de cacao is not Yiddish."

"Well, what is it?"

*"Cacao* is Spanish for *cocoa."*

Oh no! She should have known. Coffee, cocoa, beige—The Hat's favorite colors, of course. Sarah's mother said that Hattie was the first person she had ever heard of who had painted a wall in her apartment brown.

"I don't want a crème de cacao bathroom, or plants in it either," Sarah replied firmly.

"What are you two fighting about now?" Shirley poked her head in.

"Is this kid getting bat mitzvahed?" Hattie said, pointing to Sarah, who was now pulling on her long socks beneath the covers.

"It's a little late for that. She's almost fifteen," Shirley said. "I couldn't even get her to go to Sunday school."

"Well, she's barely Jewish," Hattie said.

"What do you mean she's barely Jewish?" Shirley asked.

"She knows no Yiddish."

"Well, for heaven's sake, Hattie, she wasn't born in the Warsaw Ghetto. She was born in the Marion County Hospital in Indianapolis. What do you expect?"

"Is that what is called an assimilated Jew?" Hattie said, pointing her finger at the lump under the covers.

"Don't point at her as if she's an Untouchable or something, Hat! We are all, for your information, assimilated Jews. Just because you live in New York doesn't give you ethnic dibs."

Sarah knew what assimilation was, but what in the heck was ethnic dibs, she wondered. "Look, you guys." She surfaced from under the covers. "Forget it. I'm not going to be bat mitzvahed. I'd rather serve in the temple of Vesta. So there!" And she dove beneath the covers again, giggling raucously. "Hey!" she called out in a muffled voice. "Would someone hand me my saddle shoes?"

# Chapter Ten

"*Il fait froid, mes enfants.*" Madame Henri bustled into the classroom. "*Aujourd'hui, nous faisons le concours d'Alliance Française.*"

"*Ah, non!*" the girls chorused.

The French Alliance, a club in the city, held an annual competition. An impromptu essay on some subject was to be written. Madame entered all of her students, whether they wanted to participate or not. There was a choice of two topics from which competitors could select. One topic was usually from French culture and required a certain knowledge of things French. The second was usually something more subjective and independent of a specific knowledge of French culture. This year the first choice was to write a five-hundred- to one-thousand-word essay comparing and contrasting a writer and a painter. It could be about any French writer or painter one chose. The alternative was to write an essay about oneself. Every student in the class, including Sarah, chose to do the second essay. She knew they all would and every essay would sound identical. "*Je m'appelle _____ . Je demeure dans la ville d'Indianapolis. J'ai quatorze ans. Mon père est un _____ . Ma mère est une _____ . Blah. Blah. Blah.*"

Sarah wished she could do something different. She looked over at Elaine and wondered what the French word for proctologist was. Surely she could start her essay with something other than her name and her father's profession. It seemed to Sarah that names were mere tags anyway. Furthermore, she was always defining herself in terms of other people: her father; her sister; even, in a way, her aunt. She supposed that was a common problem for minors, but it was wearisome. Suddenly she had a thought. If that was the way things were, why not define herself in terms of a whole slew of people. The conversation of that morning came back to her. There *was* a way to begin this essay without her name. This could be really original. Sarah began to write.

*Je me considère une Juive assimilée. Je suis née à l'hôpital de Marion County à Indianapolis, et mes grandparents sont originaires de Russie. Je ne peux pas parler*—Oh, what was the French for "Yiddish"? She'd just have to write "Yiddish." It couldn't be that different. She wrote on:—*Yiddish, et je ne parle pas Hébreu, sauf quelques mots de prière. Je ne vais à la synagogue que les jours de grandes fêtes comme Yom Kippur et Rosh Hashanna. Mais je dois avouer que je ne me sens jamais près de Dieu dans un édifice public, synagogue ou église, rempli de monde. Je préfère pratiquer ma religion en privé avec ma famille. Je préfère prier seule à voix basse. Ainsi je prie à voix basse. Je ne peux pas parler la langue des Juifs. Je n'ai jamais fait ma bat mitzvah, mais j'adore les fêtes célébrées en famille comme le seder, le Hanukkah, et j'aime aussi les plats de boules de matzoh, les crèpes de pomme de terre et le poisson gefilte. Mais la chose la plus importante est que je crois en Dieu*—*à un seul Dieu. Alors, les gens disent que je suis Américaine. « Vous êtes une Juive assimilée. » Je dis oui et non. Je suis une Américaine, mais je me sens être tout simplement Juive et non assimilée. Dans mon ésprit « assimilée » suggère un Juif dilué.* (Was there such a thing as a diluted Jew? Oh well, what the heck, she wrote it anyway.) *Je ne suis pas dilué. Je crois que Jésus était un grand homme très affable, mais pour moi il n'y a qu'un Dieu. Je serais la même Juive en Israël, en*

*Russie, en Italie, en Angleterre, en Chine. Ni plus, ni moins.*
*C'est moi.*

Sarah reread her essay and translated it silently to herself.

I am an assimilated Jew. I was born in Indianapolis at
the Marion County Hospital. But my grandparents
were born in Russia. I can't speak Yiddish and only a
few words of prayer in Hebrew. I only go to the synagogue on the High Holy Days such as Yom Kippur
and Rosh Hashanna. But I must admit that I never feel
close to God in a building, either a synagogue or a
church, with lots of people. I don't like organized religion. I prefer religion in private with my family. I prefer
to pray alone in a low voice. Thus I pray in a low voice.
Therefore, I do not speak the language of the Jews. I
was never bat mitzvahed. But I do love all the family
celebrations like the seder and Hanukkah, and I like the
food—matzoh balls, potato pancakes, and gefilte fish.
But the most important thing is, I believe in only one
God. Okay, people then say, you're an American. You
are an assimilated Jew. I say yes and no. I am an American but I really feel that I am just a plain Jew. The
word *assimilated* suggests a diluted Jew. I am not diluted. I believe that Jesus was a great man, a pleasant
man, but for me there is only one God. I would be the
same Jew in Israel, in Russia, in Italy, in England, in
China. Nothing more, nothing less. That's me.

# Chapter Eleven

"*Au revoir. A bientôt.*" Madame bid the girls good-bye as they handed in their essays and filed out.

French to ancient history—it was an abrupt shift in gears. Miss Ullrich, a mountainous woman, sat behind her cluttered desk. She rarely got up. When she needed to indicate something on a map, she would pick up an exceedingly long pointer and wave it in the general direction of the continent and/or geographic area in question—Mesopotamia, the Holy Roman Empire, whatever. A hook was affixed to the end of the pointer so she could pull down maps as she needed them. If there was a mechanical problem—a map that refused to descend or perhaps fell down completely —a student was called upon to fix it. Despite Miss Ullrich's sedentary habits she was intensely excited by history and on occasion absolutely spewed with volcanic enthusiasm over some point. She was at the moment gesticulating wildly. A large map made by an ardent student of some previous decade had been pulled down.

"What you see here," Miss Ullrich boomed, "is a map, a chart, of the island and surrounding waters of Salamis, Greece. You see Salamis is separated from Attica by a narrow channel leading into the Bay of Eleusis over here. This channel is divided by the island of Psyttalea."

Bay of Eleusis. Psyttalea. These words of locus tumbled off Miss Ullrich's tongue as easily as street names of downtown Indianapolis. She was thoroughly conversant with the ancient world.

Set her down in fifth-century-B.C. Rome, Athens, Alexandria, and she would find her way around as easily as she would find her way from L. S. Ayre's to the William H. Block Company, the two main department stores in downtown Indianapolis. She was now deeply involved in explaining the tactical maneuvers of the Battle of Salamis; how the Greeks, with severe losses at Thermopylae, including the death of the heroic Leonidas, were forced to withdraw south to the Bay of Salamis. Under the "masterly skill" of Themistocles they managed to induce the Persian leader Xerxes to attack under false pretenses.

It seemed to Sarah that Miss Ullrich, like so many of the teachers at Stuart Hall (except, of course, for Madame), reserved her passion for her work. And her work meant a safe, orderly life, Sarah supposed, one without chance, without adventure. Perhaps this was because, as in Miss Ullrich's case, these women were monumentally unattractive in a physical sense—despite all the old adages about beauty being only skin-deep, there were limits, especially when the skin was as deep as Miss Ullrich's. It bothered Sarah that people were so ready to spout easy lines about beauty not counting. It did count. All of her mother's friends were pretty; if they were not naturally pretty, they worked darned hard at spending their time and money to acquire an "attractive look." Parents could say all they wanted to about nobody noticing that zit if you put on a smile. No smile ever outdazzled the glow of a red zit, and no really unattractive woman ever found romance through knowing the prevailing wind directions in the Bay of Salamis in the year 480 B.C. as Miss Ullrich was now expounding.

"So you see," she continued, "although the prevailing wind was northerly, on that particular day the wind probably swung to the east, slamming the Persian fleet into the Bay of Eleusis. There was no sea room—room for maneuvering. Those ships could only sail downwind and row against it. An entire fleet rowing out of there! Mass confusion. The fleet was annihilated. I have discussed this with a friend of mine back East, Ashton Phillips, a member of the New York Yacht Club. He feels it most likely that there was a sudden wind shift. Xerxes was no dunderhead. He wouldn't have started in there in an obviously unfavorable position."

Miss Ullrich paused. She slid her spectacles up into her nest of piled grayish brown hair, anchored her hair comb over her left temple, and then, in her most patently athletic act of the day, spread out her hands, stretched her fingers apart, then clasped the hands together. These were the calisthenics that usually preceded a grand historical pronouncement. "What I want to suggest is . . ." Miss Ullrich never stated; she always "suggested." "Suggesting" gave students "sea room" to think and draw their own conclusions. She continued. "I want to suggest that had Athens and Sparta succumbed to Xerxes, to this attack of oriental despotism with all the religious mumbo jumbo—— Remember, girls, that although the Persians were highly civilized, the people, unlike the Greeks, lacked citizenship and were subject to the king and to an intellectual bondage. We all remember Darius's words in the Behistun inscription."

Sarah's mind raced back three weeks. What in the heck had been the Behistun inscription? " 'By the grace of Ahuramazda,' " Miss Ullrich intoned, " 'these lands have conformed to my decree; even as it was commanded unto them by me, so it was done.' " Miss Ullrich paused to let that sink in and to fix her comb over her other temple. Pendulous packets of flesh swung from her upper arms as she raised them to deal with the tortoise-shell comb. "As I was suggesting to you, had Greece succumbed to this orientalism, the Parthenon, the Attic Theater, the dialogues of Plato would have never come to be. It would have been as if Phidias and Sophocles and Aristotle had never been born."

Not to mention, Sarah thought, Ashton Phillips, the New York Yacht Club, Wellesley College, Juilliard, Disneyland, the 500 Mile Race, and Stuart Hall. "It was indeed because the grand heroes . . ." She paused here to stare at the girls. Her faded, tobacco-colored eyes were cold. "I truly mean grand here. Leonidas and Themistocles were just that. And their influence stretches from the fifth century before Christ to today, 1962. Our world today is different because of these two men. And although some might disagree . . ." Miss Ullrich was closing her book and reassembling her notes. She was becoming busy in the activities of drawing the class to a close, and her eyes were cast down on her desk. "I would like to suggest also that Leonidas and Themistocles, unlike some of our more popular political figures of today, are true heroes and that today we tend to pick easy heroes and we pick them too quickly." Sarah knew that she was referring to John Kennedy and his brothers. Miss Ullrich, like all the teachers except for Madame, was a rabid Republican.

"Can you believe Miss Ullrich!" Elaine Bauer fumed during the short morning recess that followed ancient history. It was too cold to go outside, so several students had gathered in the wings of the empty stage to eat their apples or whatever snacks they had. It was, of course, illegal. Food was supposed to be consumed only in the dining room or outdoors.

"What?" Hillary asked.

"What she said about easy heroes," Elaine replied.

"Who was she talking about?" Hillary's clear green eyes looked confused.

"The Kennedys, naturally," Sarah said.

"She hates the Kennedys, in case you haven't noticed," Elaine offered.

"Well, she is a Republican," Hillary said simply.

"She's right." Phoebe Buxton chimed in. "There's too much hero worship going on."

The argument had started. Sarah leaned back against some flats of scenery. Why had Elaine even brought it up? Now that Marla was gone she and Elaine were the only Democrats in the school. Within minutes the air swirled with little dirty bits of gossip: His father's a bootlegger. That's how the Kennedys made all their money. He has other women. He dyes his hair. He smokes eighty cigars a day.

This is an easy hero, Sarah thought! He certainly had no heroic stature among them. Lacey Denton had wandered backstage. "You guys aren't supposed to be back here," she warned.

"Come on, Lacey! We're having an intellectual discussion," Lisa Cody said.

"Hah!" Sarah laughed.

Lacey was perfect looking—deep honey blonde hair perfectly set, always in a long page-boy style that rolled under as it touched her shoulders. She had big, bright, blue eyes and deep dimples. "Sarah evidently doesn't think so." She spoke haughtily. But it was not the natural superiority of an upperclassman. There was an edge of real dislike in her voice.

Sarah spoke slowly. "I don't think that tearing Kennedy's character to shreds is particularly intellectual."

That was all Lacey had to hear. She plunged into the fray, offering her own sordid tidbits of information and hearsay. Sarah didn't listen. She stared out across the stage. It had been over a month since the Christmas pageant, since Lacey's understudy role as the Virgin, since her own role as a shepherd. The empty stage suddenly became peopled with figures: angels, virgins, kings, shepherds, Greek heroes, and oriental villains. But what became increasingly weird to Sarah was not the stage peopled with her imaginary figures, but the wings. Six girls in uniforms sat gossiping about one of the few people in this century who ever had a chance at becoming a hero. She looked at Lacey Denton delivering gossip like gospel.

Is this life? Sarah thought. Listening to girls tear apart people the way they did candidates for their silly social clubs? Sarah watched the stage, transformed with the imaginary figures.

There were, of course, legions of Breck shampoo girls walking about. Every single member of the Stuart Hall community who had filled out Sarah's Angel Perception Analysis survey had preferred their angels to be blonde with blue eyes. They had chosen either the platinum blonde or the one with the reddish overtones. This was also the choice of the mayor of Indianapolis and two astronauts. Kennedy and the Pope had not answered the letter. Martin Luther King had not chosen a blonde with blue eyes. Walt Disney wrote her a very nice letter, but he did not return the survey form or even mention it. The saddest thing to Sarah was that Hillary and Phoebe both believed that even shepherds should have blonde hair and blue eyes, although they had neither. Sarah had argued vehemently with them over this. She wasn't sure it mattered anymore. Admittedly it was slightly disturbing to think that there was neither a role on the stage nor in heaven for her "type." "Don't call us. We'll call you," St. Peter says as she approaches the pearly gates. Sarah continued to stare at the illusory cast.

Even Miss Ullrich was there, wandering around looking for her legendary Greek hero. She was thinner, prettier, dressed in a chiton. Sarah glanced back to Lacey. Which was more real? The stage or the wings? Suddenly she remembered Jacques's speech in *As You Like It*. They had read it earlier this year and had had to memorize the long soliloquy. "All the world's a stage, and all the men and women merely players." But all the world isn't a stage,

Sarah thought. Some of it is the wings, filled with vile-spirited girls in uniforms who never have the nerve to step onto the stage in a real part. "But make out behind tombstones of minor poets!" Sarah had risen to her feet shouting.

"Have you gone nuts?" Elaine was saying.

"No!" Sarah said in a quiet voice. Lacey Denton was white with anger. "But people like you make me puke, Lacey!" She turned on her heel and walked out.

# Chapter Twelve

"I'm starved," Sarah shouted as she and Elaine walked through the back door. Then she turned to Elaine. "I forgot my mom's not here today."

"Where is she?"

"Meals-on-Wheels. She delivers food to shut-ins, old sick people. It takes her forever in this snow, and her car's always stalling."

Ten minutes later the two girls headed for Sarah's bedroom with a tray bearing bottles of Coke, potato chips, and a plate with "brownwiches," Sarah's own invention.

"We should have a dermatologist on call," Elaine said, looking at the confection.

"Ummm! These are so good, these brownies. Wait till you taste them. You split a brownie, slather on a layer of ice cream, a layer of Junior Mints. Then the other half of the brownie, more ice cream, this time a layer of M&M's, put a second brownie on top. Freeze until solid. And there you have it—a brownwich."

"Oooh, it sounds fabulous!"

They set the tray on the floor. "Let's not even think of our ancient history reports," Sarah said, "until we've eaten."

"Food for thought," Elaine said, and bit into the brownwich. "Oh heavens! No wonder Lacey Denton doesn't have zits. She never eats stuff like this."

"Stop talking about Lacey."

"Come on, Benjamin! You did what everybody since time immemorial has been dying to do: tell off that jerk!"

"Everybody has not always been dying to do that. If that's so, how come she has so many friends?"

"Just seniors. Everybody else hates her. She's stuck-up, two-faced, and a tattletale. You're the hero of the underclassmen."

"Miss Ullrich is right," Sarah said.

"How?"

"Easy heroes."

"Come off it!"

"If I'm a hero just for telling off a stuck-up jerk like Lacey Denton, I'd rather not be a hero."

"Well, let's just say that everyone thinks it's awfully nice what you did."

The phone rang. "Oh, it's Aunt Hattie's." Sarah got up and went through the connecting bathroom into Hattie's room. She picked up the phone. "Hattie Silverman and Associates. . . . Huh? . . . Huh? Say that again. . . . NO! Put her on. . . . Lieba, what's happening? . . . Oh no, it's Greenville, not Greenfield. . . . What? Wait a minute, let me get the schedule." Sarah set down the phone.

Elaine had walked in. "What's happening?" she asked.

"Everything that shouldn't. Oh Lord!" Sarah muttered, looking at the big calendar Hattie had on the desk. "She's not supposed to be in Greenville until tomorrow anyway, but she's always arriving early at the wrong place." She picked up the phone again. "Lieba, can't you get a bus from there to South Carolina? South Carolina." Sarah repeated slowly. "Oh no." She put a hand over the receiver. "Her purse was snatched," she said to Elaine. "Okay, Lieba, quit crying. Pull yourself together. I said . . . Look, just put the policeman back on the phone. . . . Yeah, I know she's hysterical. But it is a Stradivarius. . . . What's a Stradivarius? Well, it's a very good violin. She likes to have two seats on the bus so no one next to her will bump it. . . . Listen, my aunt, her manager, isn't here right now,

96

and my mom isn't here either. I'll try and get my dad. Okay, what's your number down there? . . . Okeydokey."

Sarah set the receiver back on the phone and turned around slowly toward Elaine. "You are not going to believe this."

"Who's Lieba?" Elaine asked.

"Lieba is a violinist who arrived a year early from Bucharest and is now in Greenfield, Indiana, instead of Greenville, South Carolina, where she is supposed to be playing two dates—one at a small college, the other at a Bonds for Israel dinner. Apparently she is hysterical in the police station there and saying it is snowing too hard to get on a bus with her violin."

"Where is The Hat?" Elaine asked.

"The Hat is at some beauty camp—Last Chance, Main Chance, I don't know. Anyhow, it's in Arizona and she goes every January. They roll in mud and wear peach-colored robes. She's supposed to fly directly from Arizona to Greenville."

"And your mom is at Meals-on-Wheels. How 'bout your dad?"

"I'd better call him. Get me my Coke. I need sustenance." Sarah dialed her dad's office number. "Hi, Mrs. Nicholson, it's Sarah. Is my dad in? . . . Oh, no."

"What is it?" Elaine asked as she handed the Coke to Sarah.

"He's in the OR," she said to Elaine. "How long has he been in there, Mrs. Nicholson? . . . Oh dear! Poor thing. . . . Oh, yeah. . . . No, no. Not exactly an emergency. No, she's not home. . . . No, it's okay. Bye-bye." She hung up the phone. "They brought in some four-year-old with second- and third-degree burns over thirty percent of her body. So he's in there cutting."

"Don't they do skin grafts?"

"First they have to cut away all the burned tissue. Mrs. Nicholson said he just went in forty-five minutes ago and there's no telling how long he might be in there. I cannot believe this! What am I going to do, with everybody away? I'm so ticked off at Hattie. At least Mom and Dad are involved in life-saving activities, but Hattie is just out there in the desert getting her darned beauty treatments and here I'm left holding the bag, which contains a hysterical Rumanian violinist."

"Maybe she's calmed down. Why don't you call back?"

"I guess I should." Sarah dialed the number. It rang three times. "Hello. Uh, this is Sarah Benjamin. I'm calling— Oh. Oh, yes." Sarah put her hand over the receiver. "Hey, I'm famous in Greenfield! They knew what I was calling about even before I said— Hello, officer, yeah. . . . Yeah. . . . *What?* Oh, you gotta be kidding!"

"What is it?" Elaine was at her elbow.

"She's pregnant!" Sarah hissed. "How I'll never know. She looks just like Mozart— What? Oh. . . ." Sarah looked out the window. The snow was coming down thickly. There was no choice. She knew what she had to do. "Okay," Sarah said into the receiver, "tell the matron to give her back the Stradivarius—the violin. It's not a weapon. I'll be coming down for her. Yeah, I'll get a bus somehow. Tell her to calm down. Never mind, just put her on the phone." Sarah looked at Elaine. "Will you come with me? It's not exactly the battle of Salamis, rescuing a hysterical, pregnant, Rumanian violinist."

"Yeah, and you don't look like Themistocles, but I'll come," Elaine said.

"Lieba!" Sarah turned her attention back to the phone. "Sit tight. I mean sit down. They're going to give you back the violin. Now, don't worry. My friend Elaine and I are coming down there for you. Normally it's not a very long trip, but it might take awhile tonight because it's starting to snow pretty hard, but just calm down. . . . Oh really? In Israel. . . . Well, don't worry. It's probably not good for the baby to worry." This was ridiculous! A fourteen-

year-old giving advice on pregnancy. "We'll be there. Okay, bye."
Sarah put down the phone.

"She's really pregnant?" Elaine asked.

"Yep. She is really pregnant and she is married—to a Russian
flute player who fled to Israel and is supposed to be coming here in
the spring. Boy, is The Hat going to be mad!"

"Why?"

"Well, first of all she hates pregnant artists, especially string
players—worse than ballet dancers."

"Why?" Elaine asked.

"Why? Who knows? Who knows why Hattie ever thinks
what she thinks. With string players it's something to do with
resonance and expanding body mass—so she says. But she's really
going to be ticked off that Lieba wasn't honest with her."

"Well, maybe she'll get a flute player in the deal. It's just too
bad that Lieba doesn't play the flute and he the violin, or maybe if
he could be pregnant, since he doesn't play strings." Elaine giggled.

"If he's any good, Hattie will hold him hostage for life. Listen,
we've got to get organized. Call the bus terminal and find out the
schedule for Greenfield. What is Greenfield from downtown?
Twenty miles? Thirty?"

"Yeah, that's all," Elaine said, "but first we've got to get downtown. And look at the snow."

"I know. It's really coming down hard. We've got to dress for
this. I'm going to get our ski clothes out. I'll be right back."

Five minutes later Sarah tossed a pile of clothes onto the bed.
"Okay. Parkas, long underwear—you can wear Marla's—thermal
socks."

"What's that?" Elaine asked, pointing to a dark canvas bag.

"My dad's knapsack from World War II. He was a medic in
the paratroops."

"Your dad? You mean he actually used a parachute?"

"Yeah. He wasn't quite so plump in those days."

"Well, are we parachuting into Greenfield?" Elaine asked.

"No. But we need supplies."

"For what? Are we going to deliver a baby?"

"Don't be ridiculous, Elaine. Can't you see it's a blizzard out there? If something happens to the bus we might need food, extra dry clothes. I've got to bring warm stuff for Lieba to wear. You can't believe how she dresses. She looks like a total idiot. Oh, and I must bring several plastic bags for the violin."

"Doesn't she have a case?"

"Yeah, but this will be double protection."

"And what's that?" Elaine said pointing to a fleece-lined leather cap.

"He wore this under his helmet, I think. Isn't it neat?" Sarah put it on. The flaps hung down over her ears.

"You look like Amelia Earhart."

"Don't knock it. It's warm. I should write a note to my parents explaining all this and where we've gone."

"I'd better call mine," Elaine said.

"Will your mom object to your going?" Sarah asked.

"Yes."

"Then don't call. I'll tell my mom to call yours in my note."

On their way out the door, they stopped in the kitchen and grabbed a couple of oranges and a few cookies and crackers, which they stuffed into the knapsack. Fifteen minutes later they were tromping across the Kessler Boulevard bridge. "This snow is really heavy," Sarah said. "I hope the buses are running."

"Well, the city buses will be, I'm sure," Elaine said. "So first we just have to get to Fifty-sixth Street."

"We're walking faster than these cars are going. We should be there in fifteen minutes."

They were there in exactly fifteen minutes. They had to wait another quarter hour until the bus came.

"My hands are the only cold part, really," Sarah said, doing a little jig on the corner and slapping her mittens together.

"Here it comes!"

It took the bus one hour to negotiate the usual twenty-minute route downtown.

"No direct bus to Greenfield tonight, girls," said the man behind the ticket-counter grate at the bus station.

"Oh no!" They both moaned.

"Big semi overturned on Route 40, blocking everything up."

"Well, is there an indirect bus to Greenfield?"

"Yes, but it will take going round the barn to get there."

"Which barn?" Sarah asked wearily.

"Well, New Palestine, Morristown, Rushville. If Route 3 is open . . ." The clerk ran down all the possible ways of getting to Greenfield.

"All right, which bus?" Sarah asked.

"Number eighty-two. The one that usually goes to Rushville."

"Okay."

"You folks look prepared." He chuckled.

Sarah and Elaine climbed aboard Greyhound bus number 82. There were only three other passengers—a middle-aged woman, her hair in pin curls under a scarf, a young man in a National Guard uniform, and a man in his sixties wearing a heavy wool jacket and big work boots with bits of straw stuck to them. Sarah and Elaine headed to the rear of the bus and found a seat.

"Okay, folks." The bus driver swung up the stairs. "Everybody going to Greenfield here?"

"No. I'm going to Rushville," the young guardsman told him.

"Rest for Greenfield?"

"Yes," Sarah and Elaine and the other two passengers said.

"Well, the road's supposed to be pretty clear. I don't think we'll have any trouble."

The driver sat down. The bus started. Sarah felt a little surge of excitement deep within her gut. How silly, she thought. This would hardly qualify as an adventure. Adventures are supposed to take place in distant and exotic lands with people in safari clothes; there are big stakes like diamonds and jewels, shadowy characters like KGB spies. This is nothing but a Greyhound bus heading east out of Indianapolis. Still, the excitement was there. This was not the stage at Stuart Hall, nor was it the wings. In the thick snow the streetlamps were mere blurred swirls of light. Sarah pressed her face close to the glass. The world was transformed. Familiar buildings and streets seemed enveloped in a gossamer web of magic and silence. Fire hydrants wore snug little domed caps of white fluff. Telephone lines, cables, and wires laden with snow became the solid tracery against the night through which the snow made its silent descent upon the Midwest. Sarah remembered seeing Impressionist paintings comprised of millions of dots at the museum in Chicago. It seemed to her that as the snow dropped it fell like the dots of paint from a pointillist's brush and transformed the city she knew so well into a rare and beautiful place full of silence and whiteness. In a hospital a few blocks west her father was working, snipping away charred flesh from a child who might be dying. Her mother was navigating her yellow Corvair loaded with nutritionally balanced meals for aged and lonely people. Tonight Sarah, too, was heading someplace, to do something serious.

# Chapter Thirteen

Sarah wasn't sure how long she had been dozing when she felt the bus slow down. She opened her eyes and looked out the window. "Wow! It looks like Tibet!"

"It isn't," Elaine said. "It's Morristown, Indiana."

The bus had stopped in front of a W. T. Grant's five-and-dime. A blast of frigid air swept in as the driver opened the door. A lone woman got on. Her wool scarf was encrusted with a mantle of snow. She wore glasses that fogged as soon as she stepped into the aisle. She took the seat just behind the driver. The bus pulled out.

"Look," said Elaine. "That sign." She pointed out the window. There was a sign with an arrow pointing north beside the word CARTHAGE. "Did you even know there was a Carthage, Indiana?"

"Nope. And I'm awfully glad Aunt Hattie didn't book Lieba there."

"How come?"

"Because we'd probably be on our way to Phoenicia to retrieve her."

Elaine laughed hard at this. "Hey, Benjamin," she said suddenly. "This is totally crazy, but I had this really funny idea."

"What's that?"

"Supposing Lieba turns out to be a KGB secret agent."

Sarah's eyes flew open. "You must be kidding!"

"I think it's a terrific idea. Why not? You said she arrived a year early."

Sarah rolled her eyes. "What does that have to do with it? Believe me, Lieba Pinececsu is the last person on earth the Russians would ever pick for a spy mission. I mean, she's a total hysteric except, apparently, when she's playing."

"What do you mean, Benjamin? It's the perfect cover—a hysterical violinist."

"Don't be ridiculous, Bauer."

"No, listen, you said she didn't want to part with her violin. Maybe she's got secret documents in it, or a suicide pill."

"Well, if she's a KGB agent and has a suicide pill, I wish she had taken it, because this is one big schlep to Greenfield."

"What's a schlep?"

"Yiddish for 'dragged-out trip.' And we're schlepping to Greenfield to rescue a maiden in distress, not a communist spy."

"Damsel, maybe; maiden, no. Once you've done it, you're not a maiden, and definitely you are not one when you're pregnant."

"Unless, of course, it's the big I.C."

"Immaculate Conception, are you kidding?" Elaine hooted. "You've got Lacey Denton on the brain."

"Hardly. I just thought I'd toss the idea out. I mean maiden, matron, virgin, spy, why not? But honestly, I think there is a better chance at her being the victim of an immaculate conception than of her being a spy."

"I wouldn't be so sure about that," Elaine said. "If not a suicide pill or documents in the violin case, how about a bomb?"

"What's she going to bomb, the Bonds for Israel dinner?" Then Sarah gulped. "Holy moley!"

"What is it?"

Sarah felt her forehead begin to perspire. "You know the Russians are anti-Israel, and she said over the phone that her boyfriend—I mean husband—the flute player is in Israel."

"I'm not sure if you could fit a bomb into a flute case."

"I mean . . ." Sarah paused. "Oh, it just couldn't be true. I think we're overtired," Sarah said firmly. "We're letting our imaginations run away with us."

"Well, who's going to be at the Bonds for Israel dinner—Golda Meir? Ben Gurion?"

"Oh no. Probably just a bunch of Jewish plastic surgeons and proctologists. And George Jessel. And, oh, I think Moshe Dayan is going to be there. He's the keynote speaker. It said so on Hattie's program.

"Who are George Jessel and Moshe Dayan?" Elaine asked.

"George Jessel is a not-so-funny Jewish comedian. Moshe Dayan is even less funny—an Israeli minister and a military leader."

"See! A perfect target!" Elaine exclaimed.

"Boy, Aunt Hattie is really going to blow a gasket when she hears about all this. Gosh. And Aunt Hattie has her booked solid starting a year from now in New York, Philadelphia, Boston!"

"I wonder when the little spylet is due," Elaine said.

"Spylet? Come off it, Elaine. You're letting yourself get carried away with this thing."

"You're the one who got nervous about the Bonds for Israel dinner."

"Look, even if Lieba is a spy, it's not nice to include the baby. You know that thing they always say about the sins of the parents and the children?"

"What thing?"

"Oh, you know. The sins of the parents, not loading them on the kids or whatever."

"You mean it'll be just a cute little red baby." Elaine giggled. "When is it coming?"

"I don't know. I saw her just before Christmas and she didn't look pregnant at all. What time is it anyway?"

"Seven-thirty."

"I'm starved again."

"Well, you packed plenty of food."

"It's supposed to be for an emergency," Sarah said.

"We can eat just a little, save the rest for later. Lieba can always take her suicide pill."

"You are terrible, Elaine."

Their progress had slowed to a snail's pace as visibility diminished to only a few feet and the wet snow made the highway slicker. But finally at eight-fifteen they pulled into Greenfield.

As the girls got off the bus, they asked the driver about the return trip.

"I'm heading back to Indianapolis in twenty minutes. Think you can be on board by then?" asked the driver.

"Sure," Sarah said. "Where's the police station?"

"One block down the street that way," he said, pointing directly ahead.

How could they ever have thought the pathetic bundle on the bench could have been a KGB spy, Sarah wondered.

"Sarah!" she cried. Clutching her violin case, Lieba ran across the floor in her stocking feet. She covered Sarah's cheek with smoochy wet kisses. Sarah felt the brush of fine frizzled hair against her skin. Aunt Hattie should be drowned in an herbal mud bath! Lieba stood back. With her rounded belly and her dark eyes glistening with fear and sadness, she was the most vulnerable-looking person Sarah had ever seen; yet within her frail frame another life grew. She was so dark and small and round. She was, Sarah thought, like a planet that had lost its sun and drifted away from its galaxy, floating eerily at the edge of a universe.

"Come on, Lieba," Sarah said softly, taking her hand. "This is my friend Elaine. We'll take you home now."

"I have not any shoes. They fall apart from snow."

"We have some extras she can use," a woman police officer said.

"And I brought some socks and other warm things in this knapsack. But we've got to hurry. The bus is leaving in fifteen minutes."

"Okay. Okay, I hurry. Here, you keep this, Sarah." And she handed her the violin case.

"Well, she sure trusts you with that fiddle," the woman said. "Had a fit when I touched it."

Lieba followed the policewoman to the ladies' room.

"Aren't you at least going to look in the case?" Elaine asked.

"Oh, Elaine!" Sarah paused. "Okay." She walked over to the bench and set the case down and opened it. There were no bombs, no suicide pills, no secret documents—just one of the finest musical instruments ever made. The wood, with its dark reddish luster, seemed to possess an intrinsic radiance, probably because its every part, its very being, had been created with a dedication to expressing the most beautiful sounds conceivable.

The Stradivarius violins made in the seventeenth century now cost tens of thousands of dollars; for a young artist to own one was almost unheard-of. Hattie had helped to finance more than one Strad in her life. She did not, however, have the kind of money to underwrite an entire violin. For Lieba she had managed to borrow one, and two of Hattie's "continental" friends, a Rothschild and someone in England, had financed the insurance policy. As Sarah blinked at the instrument she realized how serious her mission really was. There was no one here in Greenfield, Indiana, except Sarah and her best friend, and together they had to get a seventeenth-century violin, a virtuoso violinist, and an unborn child safely back to Indianapolis, through a howling blizzard. Sarah closed the case carefully. Lieba emerged from the rest room, bundled up and wearing an old pair of state trooper's boots.

"Okay, guys," Sarah said. "Let's move it!" She felt once more that illusive twinge of excitement as she walked out of the police station with her hand firmly on Lieba's elbow. A blast of snow scoured her face, but her ears were warm under the fleece-lined flaps. As she tucked her chin into the collar of her parka, Sarah smiled a secret smile, knowing that although she was scared, this might be the happiest night of her life.

# Chapter Fourteen

$S$arah, Lieba, and Elaine were the only passengers that storm-laced night. This time they sat up near the driver. Ray Emmett was his name. He was from Southport, Indiana. He had been driving fourteen years, since just after the war.

The bus shimmied a little on the glazed highway.

"Don't worry, girls. I've driven through worse than this. Would you believe I've driven through a tornado?"

"You're kidding," Sarah said. "How do you drive through a tornado?"

"Fast."

Sarah had a vivid image of the Greyhound being swirled up like Dorothy's Kansas farmhouse in *The Wonderful Wizard of Oz*. She imagined Ray stepping off the bus afterward, looking around, patting a fender as the Munchkins approached, and saying, "Gee, Old Number Eighty-two, I guess we're not in Indiana anymore."

"What is it that brought you girls out on a night like this?" Ray asked.

"Kind of a rescue mission," Elaine said.

"Oh, your friend there with the fiddle?"

"Ya. Ya." Lieba nodded cheerfully. "They very nice girls, Sarah and Elaine."

"You a professional fiddler?" Ray asked.

Lieba directed a blank look at Sarah, who was sitting next to her.

"She's an artist," Sarah said. "A very well-known concert

violinist. She was en route to her next performance."

"Sakes alive!" Ray exclaimed. "You joshing me?" Ray slapped his thigh. Sarah wished he would not do that. She preferred him to have both hands on the wheel. The road was slick. The visibility was getting worse. "I got a famous person on my bus!" he said gleefully. "Most famous person I had before you was the Big O."

"The Big O?" Elaine said.

"Yeah, Oscar Robertson."

"Who Oscar Robertson?" Lieba asked.

"He's a great basketball player," Sarah replied. "He went to Crispus Attucks High School in Indianapolis."

"Yep," Ray said. "The Big O and his aunt got on this bus in Connorsville one afternoon. Sakes that boy's big! Had to hunch way over with his legs in the aisle. His aunt's just a mite of a thing." Ray paused. "What's your name, dear?"

"Lieba Pinececu."

"What? Run that by me one more time."

"Lieba Pinececu," she repeated.

"My goodness, what kind of a name is that? Foreign, I guess."

"Yes," said Lieba. "I come from Bucharest."

"Oh yeah, they do have odd names over there. Isn't that where Zsa Zsa Gabor comes from? Someplace in Hungary?"

"Not Hungary!" Lieba nearly roared. "They barbarians. I from Rumania!"

"Oh sorry! Rumania." Ray leaned forward. "Sakes this visibility is terrible. Well, girls, under regulation number six of the Greyhound safety code, if the driver deems conditions too hazardous to continue, it is his responsibility to pull his vehicle over and cease operation as soon as he can safely do so. A few hundred feet up I think there is a spot. I'm going to pull off. I don't think we'll have to stop for long. Things will improve soon enough."

Ray eased the bus to a turnout. Outside, the night swirled

white, obliterating every feature. They could have been in a plane flying through solid banks of cumulus clouds except that they could hear the whistle of the wind wrapping itself around the bus. Occasionally a few bits of snow swirled in through a tiny sliver of an opening where the door did not seal perfectly.

"Well, here we be!" Ray got up and stretched. "Let's see what we got here." Ray bent down and pulled out a lunchbox from under his seat. "Oh great! The wife packed me some chicken sandwiches. There's enough to share here if we divide them up."

"And we have some stuff, too," Sarah said, opening her dad's knapsack.

"Hey, look!" said Ray. "She put in two packages of Ho-Ho's."

"Ho-Ho's?" asked Lieba.

"Why my goodness!" Ray exclaimed. "I bet they don't have Ho-Ho's in Rumania. You don't know what you've been missing. They're chocolate hot-doggy-shaped things with cream inside."

Sarah brought out the oranges, what was left of packages of peanut butter crackers, and the last of the Fortnum and Mason cookies that Hattie had ordered for them this year.

Ray held one of the little cookies between two thick fingers. It was a cocoa-colored, star-shaped creation with a glazed cherry in the middle, a Jewel of the Punjab. "Dainty little thing, isn't it?" Ray said. "Not what you call real substantial." He popped the cookie into his mouth. "But good! How do you like the Ho-Ho's, Lieba?"

"Ummm. Verry good. I like." Lieba had just swallowed her last bite.

"You ever play that fiddle outside a concert hall?" Ray paused, and then added, "Like on a bus, for instance?"

A warm smile broke over Lieba's face. "Sure!" Her eyes glowed. "You never hear concert violinist, Ray?"

"Nope. Never."

Lieba stood up. She opened the case and took out the violin

111

and bow. She stood in the aisle and tuned ever so briefly. Then came a soft, distant glow of sound. Slowly it filled the bus, first with the warm, burnished tone of a dark-hued adagio, then the silvery quick strokes of an allegro. Sarah felt the music envelop them. She was not sure, but she thought that Lieba was playing Paganini, whose compositions Marla had told her were the most complex and challenging of violin pieces. She'd said they were often thought of as display pieces because they were replete with difficult passages, demanding and striking effects, that required technical wizardry. Hattie complained that too many young artists took on Paganini merely to master stunts and came out like automatons or stunt violinists. But not Lieba. Her virtuosity was beyond stunts and tricks. She had discovered the color of the music. Now as she played an incredible left-handed pizzicato of descending scales and arpeggios with finger-tearing action, the inside of the bus seemed to be adazzle in a cross fire of light and sound. The three listeners felt themselves swept up into an extraordinary musical confidence.

The wind seemed to lessen. In the distance they could hear the *huff* of the snowplows. Visibility improved and Ray went back to the wheel. Lieba sat down again but continued to play. Now the luminous tones of a Brahms concerto filled the bus. By the time they drove past Carthage, Lieba had reached the cadenza, the extended virtuoso section at the end of the first movement. The air flashed with fast-moving swoops and arcs of sound. Then the flourishes dissolved into the thrilling slow phrases at the beginning of a new movement. A purity Sarah had never heard before came from the violin. As the bus made its way through the stormy Indiana night, Sarah felt herself and the others swept deeper and deeper into Lieba's confidence. That indeed was the heart and soul of Lieba's virtuosity—to make personal the art. For against the storm, or perhaps within it, at its very eye, was this conspiracy of music!

# Chapter Fifteen

When they finally reached downtown Indianapolis the girls found that the city had literally been brought to a standstill by the blizzard. The telephone lines were out and there was bus service only to Forty-sixth Street. From there on, they would be on their own. But the sky had cleared and the wind had dropped, and the night seemed much warmer. When the three descended from the bus at Forty-sixth and Meridian, Sarah was optimistic that within forty-five minutes they would be home. They checked Lieba's suitcase at the Greyhound station and started out. The sidewalks were un-walkable, but a narrow lane had been plowed down Meridian. There were no cars, so the girls took to walking down the center of the street. Lieba seemed quite enthusiastic and ready for the hike. The music had restored her and she chattered away in her broken English about summer hikes in the Carpathian Mountains.

Between the two of them, Sarah and Elaine must have known at least ten families who lived in the stately old Tudor and Georgian brick homes that lined Meridian. Any one of these families would have gladly welcomed the girls, but that would have ruined every-thing. It was almost as if there was an unspoken pact between them: no grown-up help allowed. For although the object of their trip was to get Lieba, the unborn child, and the Stradivarius to safety, there was a certain style in which it had to be accomplished. And that style did not include standing in friends' homes melting snow on their oriental carpets. Rather, they would walk alone and free in the muffled white starlit world with the music still playing within them.

They walked briskly. "I can't believe it," said Elaine. "We're at Fifth-sixth Street already. Should we turn here or wait till Kessler?"

"Wait," said Sarah. "Who knows whether Illinois has been plowed at all."

So they strode on and several minutes later turned left onto Kessler Boulevard. They walked a few blocks and came to the bridge that crossed the White River. The bridge road had not been plowed, and a thick billowy blanket of snow lay on it like a down quilt.

"Look at the bridge!" Sarah said. "It looks like a giant bed."

"Oooh! And I'm ready to flop on it," said Elaine. She walked out onto the bridge and fell backward. "It's so soft. This feels neat!"

"I'm going to make a snow angel," Sarah said as she flopped down ahead of Elaine.

"What's that?" Lieba asked.

"Watch," Sarah said, and she began swinging her arms up and down at her sides. Then she stepped carefully out of the angel impression she had made in the snow.

"Ah-ha! So pretty! Hold please my violin," Lieba said, handing the plastic-bagged case to Sarah. "I want to try this thing." She lay down and began to swing her arms.

"Great!" shouted Sarah. "Hey, I've got an idea. Let's make a chain of angels going right down the middle of the bridge."

"Oh terrific!" Elaine said.

So the girls began pressing in their angel prints in turn. Sarah and Elaine took turns holding Lieba's violin when she made hers. Sarah made the last print at the west end of the bridge. She looked up at the stars that chinked the winter night. The whole Milky Way galaxy gleamed across the sky. Earth was really so tiny, Sarah

114

thought, an infinitesimal speck of light. Yet, who knew? In someone else's vision earth might shine like a star. She wondered if there were such things as angels, or if there was other more tangible life out there in space. And if there was, she hoped those beings had music like Brahms, and an artist like Lieba to play it, and clean, deep snow and cold, starry nights. This was Sarah's wish, her prayer for outer space.

# Chapter Sixteen

Dear Marla,

I suppose you've heard by now of the great Lieba rescue mission. Dad said that when I showed up at the back door I looked just like Sergeant Preston of the Yukon and Elaine and Lieba looked like the huskies. He's always going around now shouting "Mush, you huskies! Mush!"

Now get this! Guess who won the *Alliance Française concours d'essai? Moi! Votre-même vraiment* (Yours truly). Mom was so excited that she tried to call you before the rates go down (That's really excited for her. What if she knew that's practically the only time I call you!) Anyhow, you weren't in. Obviously. I shouldn't waste space in a letter telling you you weren't in. You know that, right? My essay was on being an assimilated Jew. *Juive assimilée.* Weird? Definitely. It was all I could think to write about. Dad wants to send a copy to Rabbi Gordon. I don't want him to, because I'm scared they—the temple—will come after me and try to rope me into some religious activity or one of those loathesome Temple Teen groups where you have to go on retreats and contemplate your heritage, play volleyball, eat cafeteria food, and sleep in bunk beds.

As a matter of fact, this award is getting to be a pain in the neck. Mom keeps saying I'm so good in French I should take my college boards in it. (That, of course, is only two years off. Never can plan too far ahead!) Aunt Hattie says if I were only musical I could go to Paris and study with Nadia Boulanger. As an alternative she suggested we go to Paris for the High Holy Days next year. She knows a "darling" synagogue on the *Rue* something or other. I, of course, could translate the service. Dad said he'll be damned if he's going to Paris in order to fast on Yom Kippur. Needless to say, this has raised everybody's hopes for *votre-vraiment* to a dangerous level. I might have to become a juvenile delinquent to correct the impression and lower the expectation level. What's worse is that we all have to attend a dinner downtown when they give me and three other high school students who won in other categories, our medals and I have to make a thank-you speech. Not just *"merci"* either, but thirty seconds' worth of *merci*. Madame, God bless her—or rather, *Dieu beni-elle*—says she'll help me with it, which really means she'll write it for me.

The Hat is in town this week. Hallelujah! Ha! Ha! Ha! She wasn't as ticked at Lieba as I thought she would be. She's going to let Lieba live in her apartment, after the person who is there now gets out. She'll stay there until the baby comes, in July. Lieba's husband is supposed to be coming from Israel in June. He's a flutist, and Isaac Stern is his sponsor. So Hattie has been on the phone constantly with Stern and somebody in Tel Aviv. She's trying to, as she put it, do "an end run" around Sol Hurok and sign up Shlomo (Yes, that's his name!) Rabinowitz. You should hear her conversations with Shlomo. All he wants to talk about is Lieba and the baby. All The Hat wants to talk about is Shlomo and dates at Avery Fisher Hall in New York. If he doesn't sign with her, she'll probably hold the baby hostage. Even though Lieba looks like a total freak she's really nice, and when she plays the violin—well, Marla, there is nothing like it. You actually do forget about her hair, and I don't often forget about hair. I never thought I would be quoting Aunt Hattie, but honest to gosh you wouldn't care if she were bald. I told Lieba that I hope the baby comes on the Fourth of July—they could

117

name it Liberty Bell. Guess what? She loves the name! She loves everything American. I guess it seems sort of exotic to her. Maybe if we were having babies in Russia or Rumania we'd be naming them Borscht Benjamin or something. So anyhow, come summer, we might be welcoming little Liberty Bell Rabinowitz.

School is sooooo borrrring! I have to think up something to do for my darned ancient-history report. I've been thinking about doing something on vestal virgins in ancient Rome. They really are kind of neat. And there's a lot of gross stuff that would really be fun to write about. Like for instance, did you know that they were entombed alive if they were found with a man—not just sitting there beside him, but making out with him or something. Aunt Hattie thinks I ought to do a kind of TV-interview-style report like that program "You Are There" with Edward R. Murrow. You know how Murrow goes down to the dock and interviews Columbus just before he sets sail for the New World. Or I remember a few years ago he interviewed Paul Revere when he was waiting for the one-if-by-land-two-if-by-sea signal. Well, The Hat thinks I should write an interview with a vestal virgin who is about to be walled up. It's a nice idea, but I'm not sure Miss Ullrich will go for it. Also, how do you start the interview? So far all I've written is the introduction. Ed is standing outside the tomb. "Good evening, ladies and gentlemen, I'm Edward R. Murrow, your host this evening. I'm standing here just west of the Cataline Hill by a tomb. Beyond this tiny door sits a young woman, a guardian of the temple of Vesta. She is composed, even serene, one might say, and yet in a matter of moments she shall be sealed in this stone cell for eternity. She has been found guilty of the worst crime imaginable for a guardian of the temple of Vesta. She has violated her sacred oath. She was found making out with a man. For this she must be buried alive. We are now going to enter the tomb for a brief few minutes and interview

Miss Fabia Livonis, vestal virgin. The year is 54 B.C., the place Rome—and You Are There!"

But now I can't think of any questions. I mean, Murrow can't just go in there and say, "Gee, Fabia, was it worth it, making out with Drusus Augustus Marcellus?" Mom says I should just write a straight report. Here's what Mom calls a straight report. Get this for an opening sentence. "Had she lived in the year 54 B.C. Lacey Denton would have been unacceptable as a guardian of the temple of Vesta." Then she and The Hat and Dad just hoot and slap their knees. Between Dad and his Sergeant Preston jokes and Mom and her vestal virgin ones, I'm being driven nuts and this report isn't getting written. So, if you have any ideas please write or call immediately. If you could just think up the first couple of questions for me to have Murrow ask, I know I'd be off and running.

How's everything going with you? What are you working on now? Still the Schumann? Did you know your piano teacher wrote Mom and said you were the light of her day, the something else in her heart, and there was some other body part mentioned. Anyway, she thinks you're great.

> Love and xxxxxxxxxxx
> *Votre-même vraiment,*
> The prodigy's younger sister,
> Sarah, *la Reine du Yukon*

P.S.   The Hat still wants to paint the bathroom crème de ca-ca.

# PART III

## NOVEMBER 1962

# Chapter Seventeen

" 'And it came to pass in those days, that there went out a decree from Caesar Augustus, that all the world should be taxed. (And this taxing was first made when Cyrenius was governor of Syria.) And all went to be taxed, every one into his own city. And Joseph also went up from Galilee, out of the city of Nazareth, into Judea, unto the city of David, which is called Bethlehem. . . .' "

"When is it that we have to get up and walk across the stage?" Libby Dyer asked. She was a new shepherd. There were five this year instead of four.

"Not for a while," Sarah told her. "The Virgin has to sing her lullaby, and the angels have their bit. The chorus sings the shepherd song and that's our cue. Then we get up and go."

"Oh gosh, I'm so nervous," Libby whispered.

"Nervous?" Elaine said. "This is the easiest thing you'll ever have to do in your entire life."

"That shows you the difference between a freshman and a junior," muttered Phoebe Buxton. "Just wait till you have to take the PSAT. Now, that's something to be nervous about."

"Oooh! This time next year," Sarah said softly.

"Were they really that bad, Phoebe?" Elaine asked.

"Let's just say I'd take being a shepherd any day of the week over taking the PSAT."

"You know Susie Lester's cousin Colin?" Elaine asked.

"Yeah," said Phoebe. "What does he have to do with anything?"

"His dad went to Princeton and so did his brother and grand-father and uncle. He did lousy on the PSAT and the SAT, and no way was he getting into Princeton on those scores. He kept taking them and taking them till he couldn't stand it anymore. So——"

"Don't tell me," Sarah interrupted. "He's a shepherd in Galilee now!"

"No. Not so lucky. It's awful. He joined the army."

"What's so awful about the army?" Phoebe asked.

"They sent him to that weird-sounding country—Vat something."

"Viet Nam," Sarah said.

"Yeah, that's the one. Where is it?"

"I don't know," Phoebe said.

"Me neither," Libby said softly. "Faraway, I think."

"Near the orient somewhere, maybe," said Sarah. "It could be exotic, exciting—better than Princeton."

"No." Elaine shook her head. "There's a war going on."

"A war!" Sarah turned onto her side. "Watch that crook, Buxton! I never heard about any war over there."

"It's a quiet one," Elaine said.

"Must be very quiet," Sarah said. "Is he actually fighting in it?"

"No, they call him an adviser. He flies around in an airplane and tells the pilot where to drop bombs. But he had to go to language school and learn whatever language it is they speak over there." Miss Crowninshield had paused in her narration. In the lull, Elaine's voice dropped to a whisper.

"Oh gosh, that does sound awful," Sarah said. "At least with the PSATs you don't die if you get the wrong answer."

"It's terrible," whispered Hillary. Her head was somewhere near Sarah's ear, and Sarah could feel a warm, tremulous stream of breath on her cheek. "I wonder where they drop the bombs."

123

"I don't know," said Elaine. "Towns, villages, I guess."

"How horrible!" whispered Hillary.

The Virgin had just begun to sing the lullaby: "Ooohh lay thou little tiny child/Bye, bye, ooh lee ooh lay. . . ."

Did bombs ever hit babies? Sarah wondered.

Backstage after rehearsal, the shepherds were hanging up their robes. Elaine had just finished taking off her burnoose and was attempting to comb her hair in a fragment of mirror that was propped near the bank of electrical switches. Sarah hung up her own robe, watching Elaine. It seemed she was always primping now. Makeup was not allowed in school. It was one of the ten thousand rules that governed their lives. The no makeup rule was part of a subsection on appropriate dress. There was, of course, only one appropriate dress: the school uniform, a navy blue serge jumper to be worn with a white shirt. In addition, no colored socks were permitted (other than white, navy, black, or gray) and no excessive jewelry.

Crucifixes and Stars of David were considered not excessive, as were mustard seeds enclosed in crystal spheres and suspended from chains. Circle pins that were bland gold rings about an inch in diameter could also be worn. Hair ribbons were acceptable, but "under no circumstance" could Indian-style headbands be worn, and certainly no eye makeup. It had always intrigued Sarah that the Indian headband rule and the eye makeup one were right next to each other. Sarah imagined that Miss Crowninshield had been thinking about Indians when she wrote the rule and then she "naturally" thought of war paint, thus the rule about eye makeup. In Crowninshield's twisted way of thinking she had probably thought "Indians–savages–war-paint–makeup–sex" in just the same way she thought "angels–pure–white–blonde."

In spite of all these rules, Elaine and several other girls found plenty to do to their appearance. Elaine carried tweezers to "maintain" the arch of her eyebrows and quickly dispatched any errant hairs that showed up not only outside the immediate shadow of the arch but, heaven forbid, on her chin or some other such horrendous location. She also carried Vaseline in a tiny jar and applied it to her eyelashes. This was supposed to encourage luxuriant growth in what was just a pale, thin fringe of brownish hairs. She also carried a tube of flesh-toned Erase. Erase did not constitute makeup because it did not "add to" one's appearance but merely "blotted out" unslightly blemishes.

The "Erase issue" had actually occupied ten minutes of the last student government meeting. Following a question about the dress code, a sophomore had asked, "Is Erase a makeup?"

"Yes. You can live without it. It is not a health aid." So said Mrs. Forest, the librarian and a faculty counselor to student government. She was also one of the most disastrous-looking human beings alive.

"No it isn't. How can you compare Erase to mascara?" responded Hope Linden, a senior and the editor of the yearbook. "It doesn't darken or exoticize." Smith College had better accept Hope Linden, Sarah thought. They'd have a good thing coming their way.

"And it's not like lipstick," said Margery Webber. "It doesn't heighten color, redden or pinken." There was laughter over "pinken."

"Well, that's an interesting verb, Margery." Miss Hoffritz, the English teacher and other faculty adviser, was roused from her near-slumber at the back of the auditorium. "I suppose Margery is right. It does not add color. Would you say it enhances appearance?"

A four-minute semantic argument then ensued over the words *enhanced* and *add to*. The conclusion was that as long as an appearance was enhanced by blotting out or "erasing" rather than by adding color, tubes of Erase were acceptable. So now Sarah watched as Elaine erased one pimple on her forehead, two dark shadows under her eyes, and a scattering of freckles across her nose.

"Why are you going to all that trouble?" Sarah asked.

"It's no trouble," Elaine said cheerfully. "It's fun. Besides, Stephen is picking me up after school."

"That's four hours from now."

"I'll touch it up before last period."

Sarah sighed. Elaine had become excruciatingly boring since Stephen had entered her life. Sarah wondered if she should tell Elaine that she had seen Stephen at the corner of Fifty-sixth and Illinois yesterday picking his nose.

"Did you ever tell Stephen what your dad does?" Sarah asked.

"Stephen understands. He has a medical background."

"What do you mean by that?"

"His dad's a doctor."

"Oh. The way you said it, I thought you meant *he* was a doctor. Is his dad a proctologist?"

"No. A psychiatrist."

"That really doesn't count," Sarah said.

"What do you mean it doesn't count?" Elaine looked away from the mirror for the first time. "How can you dismiss a major part of the medical profession?"

"Easy," Sarah said. "Anyhow, being a psychiatrist is about as far as you can get on the body from your father's area of expertise. Unless, of course, you 'shrink' up the body." Sarah cracked up over her own pun.

"Oh, you're a real hoot, Sarah Benjamin!" Elaine said, leaning closer to the mirror as she homed in underneath her right eyebrow with her tweezers. "I don't have to explain medical terms." She deftly plucked the hair. "*Seventeen* magazine says always pluck from

126

the underneath side of your eyebrow. Never on top. Your arches will collapse."

"I thought collapsing arches was feet."

"No—eyebrows, too."

Sarah continued to scrutinize Elaine as Elaine scrutinized herself, bringing her face still closer to the mirror as she became totally absorbed in the minuscule patch of skin under the crescent eyebrow. Was she jealous of Elaine? Sarah wondered. How could she be jealous of someone who had a nose-picking boyfriend? She didn't feel jealous. She didn't know what she felt. But why was Elaine staring at this tiny piece of herself? It was so boring. Elaine was such a drag. She wasn't fun anymore. Sarah wanted to scream at the top of her lungs: YOU ARE A COLOSSAL BORE! NO FUN! And in this dumb school where they made rules about the color of your socks, she needed all the fun she could get. Sarah picked up her notebook and walked through the backstage exit into a corridor. Marcy Delaney, president of student council, was posting a sheet on the announcement bulletin board.

"What's that?" asked Sarah.

"The new conduct code for the lunchroom."

"More rules? I can't believe it."

"You'd better believe it. Crowninshield will read them tomorrow in the morning announcements." Marcy stood back to look at the sheet. "She thinks we're all becoming slobs in the lunchroom, so she pushed through this new set of rules in council. Talk about puppet governments!" Marcy hissed. "I don't know why we even bother to have elections around here. All I've done in my three months as student council president is post rules made up by Crowninshield. She makes Eva Perón look like Julius Caesar."

"Who's Eva Perón?" Sarah asked.

"An Argentinian dictator—or dictatoress."

"Oh. So what are these rules anyway?" Sarah stepped up and began to read them.

## NEW LUNCHROOM BEHAVIOR CODE

1. No shuffling feet during Grace.
2. On Potato Chip Day (Tuesdays), no snacking on chips prior to Grace.
3. Milk from individual cartons is to be poured into glasses and not imbibed directly from the carton, which is a most unbecoming manner in which to drink.
4. Serving dishes are to be passed counterclockwise starting with the teacher.
5. Do not bolt food. Requests for seconds should be made only after a decent interval.
6. One and only one person should be sent to the water station for additional water, at which time a pitcher should be brought to the table. Fetching of water by individuals glass by glass causes excessive traffic and confusion at the water station.
7. Sandwiches are for Soup and Sandwich Day (Wednesdays). On other days sandwiches are not under any circumstances to be made from table bread and the meat that is being served that day.
8. Do not split the Oreo cookies. They are to be eaten whole in the form in which they were made. They are not to be split in order to scrape off the filling with teeth or tongue.
9. As always, do not sit down until the teacher at the head of your table is seated.

Sarah looked up. "You do not scrape with a tongue. You lick with your tongue and scrape with your teeth."

Marcy rolled her eyes. "You're going to make it worse than the add-or-enhance argument over Erase."

"How come there are only nine rules? It doesn't seem right."

"You mean there should be ten, the Ten Commandments of Lunchroom Behavior?"

"Yeah," Sarah said. "Ten's a nice round number. It's hard to think of Moses coming down from the mountain with only nine commandments on his tablets."

"Yeah. Like, back to the drawing board, guys!" Marcy said.

"Absolutely." Sarah laughed. Marcy was pretty nice for a student council president, even if she was just a puppet.

"Well, I'll leave that one to you, Benjamin. I've got to run."

Sarah remained, staring at the rules. What was it Marcy had said? Crowninshield was like Eva Perón? It must be very boring to be a dictator, almost as boring as being a puppet. It was the guys up in the hills—the rebels, the guerrillas—who really had all the fun. Probably Fidel Castro had really loved running around in those hills above Santiago. It was undoubtedly a lot more fun than nationalizing the banks of Havana as he had done two years before. She would never run for one of those dumb student-council jobs. She would be no one's puppet—especially not Crowninshield's. She had known this for a long time, but it wasn't until this very minute that she felt a new and strange sensation, something totally irresistible deep inside her. She knew instantly what it was. It was the warm glow, the first glimmerings, of the guerrilla in her soul.

She felt the weight of her dad's fountain pen, clipped to the V neck of her jumper. The corridor was empty. Sarah unclipped the pen and took off the cap. What could she say she was doing if she got caught? Resolutely, Sarah hunched close to the bulletin board. She wouldn't get caught, and if she did, well ... Feeling incredibly reckless, she wrote the numeral ten just below the ninth rule. Then very carefully she continued: "Do not finger the Harvard beets. It constitutes gross and unbecoming behavior for privileged girls." She capped the pen and hurried off to English class.

She slid into her seat in English. Miss Hoffritz stood in front of the class, her worn copy of *Idylls of the King* crushed against her sagging bosom, her eyelids clamped tight as she recited a passage of "Guinevere's Lament." Every November for countless years she must have stood like this, before a group of fifteen-year-old girls, and read the poet's impassioned words about imperfect love. She no longer needed to look at the book.

> "His hope he call'd it; but he never mocks, / For mockery is the fume of little hearts. / And blessed be the King, who hath forgiven / My wickedness to him, and left me hope / That in mine own heart I can live down sin / And be his mate hereafter in the heavens / Before high God! Ah great and gentle lord / Who wast, as is the conscience of a saint / Among his warring senses, to thy knights— / To whom my false voluptuous pride, that took / Full easily all impressions from below, / Would not look up, or half-despised the height / To which I would not or I could not climb— / I thought I could not breathe in that fine air, / That pure severity of perfect light— / I yearn'd for warmth and color which I found / In Lancelot—now I see thee what thou art, / Thou art the highest and most human too, . . ."

Miss Hoffritz smacked her thin lips shut and opened her eyes, which looked slightly wet. The room was silent. She seemed to stare at the faces of the girls, but Sarah realized that she was not looking at them but through them, far beyond them, as if they were not there at all. This was the way Miss Hoffritz often looked when she was reading passages about grand passion and tragic romances. She looked right through her students toward her own vision of Camelot.

"So, girls!" She sighed and with the sigh seemed to inhale her own errant spirit and return from Camelot to the sophomore English class at Stuart Hall. "Methinks the lady is too late in her realization of this highest order of love. Too late! Let's look again at some of these lines. Sally Burnham, what do you make of the lines 'I thought I could not breathe in that fine air,/That pure severity of perfect light—'?"

"Uh . . ." Three other hands shot up, but Miss Hoffritz ignored them. "Well now, Sally, what do you think Guinevere is referring to when she speaks of 'that fine air,' 'that pure severity of perfect light'? What do you think of when you hear such words?" She was trying ever so patiently to lead Sally along. "Well now, what could 'that air,' 'that severity of light,' be metaphors of? Any ideas?" She waited expectantly. Sally shifted in her seat.

"Well," Sally began. Miss Hoffritz inclined her head toward Sally. "It, uh, kind of—you know. I'm not sure this is right, but it sort of sounds like—" She stopped.

"Yes, Sally? It sounds like?"

"Switzerland?"

There was a scattered giggle throughout the room. Miss Hoffritz raised her hand to stay the giggles. " 'Mockery is the fume of little hearts'!" she reminded them. Then, ever patient: "Yes, Sally, Switzerland can have that severity of perfect light, that fine air. But we are in Camelot here, not the Swiss Alps. Now, to whom could Guinevere be likening this perfect light and fine air?"

"Arthur!" said Sally with sudden brightness.

"Yes!" It was the closest Miss Hoffritz could come to a squeal of glee. "And with whom do we associate color and warmth? For whom are these a metaphorical extension?"

"Lancelot!" Sally answered

"Absolutely!" Miss Hoffritz nodded vigorously.

"Switzerland versus Mexico," Sarah whispered.

"What was that, Sarah?"

"Oh nothing."

"Well, it must have been something. Kindly share it with us."

"Well, if King Arthur is like Switzerland with the pure light and the cold air and stuff, I just said that Lancelot must be like Mexico. You know, color and warmth."

"Oh." Miss Hoffritz coughed slightly. "Yes, I suppose one could say that. A rather odd geographic metaphor." Miss Hoffritz had a wide tolerance for most kinds of metaphorical interpretation. "But now to go back to our discussion of this highest order, this perfect kind of love which Guinevere came too late to understand. It is as if now a veil has been lifted for Guinevere. Before, she was unable to see the purity of Arthur's love. Why?" No hands went up. "Read the text, girls: '. . . false voluptuous pride, that took / Full easily all impressions from below, / Would not look up, or half-despised the height / To which I would not or I could not climb—' You see," Miss Hoffritz continued, "it was her pride, her natural inclination to look down. Her values were the base ones of materialism, naturalism; and so, girls, a defective love arose. A love that was less because it could not aspire to be more. And so we see the *Idylls*—the tragic collapse of Arthur's Round Table—as an allegory. The work is an allegory for the collapse of society and of the individual's rejection of spiritual values."

But was Miss Hoffritz thinking of Guinevere and Arthur in literary terms only? Sarah wondered. When she stared through her students to a distant land, was it really populated with allegorical figures? Admittedly, it was not populated by fifteen-year-old girls in Stuart Hall uniforms, but Sarah knew deep down that Miss Hoffritz saw *herself* in that realm of gold-spun air, but not as she was in the classroom—sixty-two years old, stooped in her baggy knit, foamy green suit, her eyeglasses hanging from a ribbon around her neck, her hair a collection of dust pussies caught under a fine hair net, her face dissolving into wrinkles and pouches. No, Sarah was sure that in those faded eyes another image glowed—a vision of a young Adele Hoffritz whose thick, lustrous hair flowed from under a pointy hat crowned with veils. She was in that "morn" they had read about in "The Coming of Arthur." Sarah flipped back in her book to the passage.

> . . . before the stateliest of her altar shrines, the king /
> That morn was married, while in stainless white, / The
> fair beginners of a nobler time, / And glorying in their
> vows and him, his knights / Stood round him, and re-
> joicing in his joy. / Far shone the fields of May through
> open door, / The sacred altar blossomed white with
> May, / The Sun of May descended on their King, / They
> gazed on all earth's beauty in their Queen, . . .

And then of course she'd gone and blown it all—Guinevere going to a nunnery where she eventually became the abbess, poor old Miss Hoffritz to live with her aging mother in an ugly, old, dusty Victorian house on Delaware Street.

No wonder Miss Hoffritz took it all so seriously, so personally. When Guinevere had messed up, she had been really upset with her. At this very moment Hoffritz was harping again on how Guinevere "perceived too late the truth." Sarah felt that Miss Hoffritz was being unduly hard on Guinevere and by implication on herself.

"Miss Hoffritz!" Sarah's hand went up

"Yes, Sarah?"

"Well . . ." Sarah paused, searching for words. "I don't know how to put this, but I think— Well, I think you're being too hard on Guinevere."

"Oh?" Miss Hoffritz put her spectacles back on. The ribbons fell in deep loops at either side of her face. "And how is that, Sarah?"

"Well, you have to admit that Guinevere is not nearly as bad as, say— What's her name? The one who killed Merlin."

"Vivian. Well, of course she's not as bad as Vivian. Few are! Vivian was the embodiment of evil."

"Well, you see," Sarah continued, "it's not even a question of how bad she was. . . ."

"Yes, I agree. It is not that Guinevere was evil." Miss Hoffritz paused. A pained look crossed her face. "It is just that her love was less than pure."

"But it's very hard to love anyone that good, Miss Hoffritz," Sarah persisted.

Miss Hoffritz looked stunned. "Do you mean Arthur?"

Sarah nodded.

"Well, Sarah, I don't really follow you. Surely, you can't mean what you just said?"

"But I do!" Sarah protested. "Arthur was impossible!"

"What do you mean, impossible?"

"As a husband. I mean he was real nice and everything and had lots of wonderful ideas—I mean ideals—the Round Table and all that. But—"

"But what? Are you suggesting, Sarah, that all women who find perfection in their mates— Should I say, rather, that this perfection being too much, should they instead seek out the Lancelots?" The other girls laughed. Miss Hoffritz smiled, enjoying their support. Sarah was mad. Here she had tried to save Hoffritz from her own delusions and now the woman was just twisting up all her words.

"No! I'm not suggesting that at all. I'm suggesting that it wasn't human, their kind of love—or at least Arthur's wasn't."

"But Sarah, the ideal, the soul, must be able to act through some earthly vessel."

Sarah supposed that she meant that Guinevere was the earthly vessel, Arthur being the ideal. "That may be true, but it's no guarantee that it will work. It can't work. It's as absurd as all that crazy business with the Holy Grail. Human love can't be a Holy Grail. You see—wait a minute. Wait!" Sarah frantically leafed through the pages of her book. "Ah!" She lifted a finger and stabbed the air. "Right here in 'The Passing of Arthur.' This is Arthur talking." Sarah began to read:

" 'I found Him in the shining of the stars,
I marked Him in the flowering of His fields,
But in His ways with men I find Him not.' "

"Yes?" Miss Hoffritz's voice was barely a whisper.

"Miss Hoffritz, he's talking about himself." Sarah didn't want to say anything more about the passage. She didn't have to. Miss Hoffritz stared right through her. Then the end-of-class bell rang.

# Chapter Eighteen

"Can you get that, sweetie? It's Hattie's phone." Sarah was sprawled on her parents' bed eating potato chips. Her mother was at her dressing table, lining a book with a yellow Hi-Liter marker.

Sarah reached the phone by the third ring. "Hattie Silverman and Associates. . . . Oh, hi, Serge. Where you calling from? London? . . . Oh, that's right. Hattie's supposed to go next week, right. Yeah. . . . Okay. Let me write it down." Sarah reached for a pencil. "Okay, a G.E., General Electric, heat lamp. Okeydokey. . . . Well, I'm okay. School is just incredibly boring. . . . They're fine. Marla's in New York. . . . Yeah, she likes Juilliard much better than Wellesley. How does Queen E. look? . . . Oh. She should have your hairdresser, Serge. Don't worry about the bald spot. What you have looks so much better than what she's got. Quality, not quantity, as they say. . . . Yeah, okay. I'll tell Aunt Hattie."

Sarah went back to her parents' bedroom.

"Who was it?" Shirley asked.

"Vronsky."

"From London? What did he want?"

"He says that the Royal Opera House still has lousy heat lamps and he wants Hattie to pick up a couple of G.E.s and bring them with her."

"Oh." Shirley buried her nose in her book.

"What are you reading, Mom?"

"*Corporate Decision-making Structures*. It's fascinating."

"Which course is it for?"

"Administration."

Sarah's mother had returned to school, and although her courses in business sounded boring to Sarah, Shirley was totally absorbed. She got *A*'s on all her papers and examinations. Sarah was actually jealous of her mother's interest and enthusiasm for school-work. She wished she found her own half so interesting.

"What's it about?" Sarah asked.

"What's what about?" Shirley looked up from her book. Sarah was now lying on the floor with her feet propped against the wall.

*"Corporate Decision-making Structures."*

"Well, in a nutshell, I'd say power is what it's about."

"Power?"

"Yep. How successful executives use it and don't abuse it in moving their companies on to better things. A kind of peek into their brains."

"Hmmm." Sarah wondered if her mother was planning to become the head of some huge conglomerate. No wonder she found her courses so stimulating. Dreams of power, dreams of manipulation, were so much more interesting than dreams of golden Camelots with maidens in pointy hats being rescued by knights. "Are any big executives female?" Sarah asked.

"Not many. But times are changing. And there have been some in the past—our own Mme. Walker, for one. She lived here in Indianapolis at one time and made a fortune in cosmetics for Negro people—especially hair-straightening formulas."

"No kidding?" Sarah said. "Who else?"

"Tillie Lewis."

"What did she do?"

"Just go to our kitchen and open the cupboards. There are all sorts of cans of Tillie Lewis tomatoes and tomato sauce."

"I'm back!" Hattie called out as she came down the hallway.

"So how was it?" Shirley asked.

"Awful!" said Hattie, flopping down in an easy chair.

"What was awful?" Sarah asked.

"Prosthetic eyeballs," Hattie said, removing her gloves. "This guy's supposed to be the best in the business, but I much prefer my little black patch to one of his 'perfectly matched' soulless orbs."

"Good for you!" Shirley said.

"So what's new?" Hattie asked.

"Vronsky called," Sarah said. "He wants you to bring two G.E. heat lamps to London."

"You mean they still haven't fixed up the physiotherapy room at the Opera House! Okay, two heat lamps, along with his pound of pastrami from the Forty-ninth Street deli and the packed-in-ice blinis from the Russian Tea Room. Well, at least heat lamps aren't fattening. How's the world of high finance?" She pulled a settee to Shirley's dressing table and sat down.

"This merger and acquisition stuff is great. Absolutely fascinating case, when American Foods made the move to take over Keystone Resorts and this fellow Bannister played tennis that morning with Gottlieb from the resorts and made an offer on 25 percent of the Keystone stock. . . ."

"Gottlieb. Gottlieb." Hattie scratched her head. "The name sounds familiar. I wonder if it could be the same Gottlieb I went out with years ago. What's his first name?"

"Ronald."

"That's it! A totally forgettable person. Quite dull, but I guess a good businessman. What have you been up to in school, toots?" she said, turning to Sarah.

"Lancelot's move to take over Guinevere and Guinevere's final merger with a convent."

Shirley and Hattie laughed. "*Idylls of the King*, I take it," Hattie said.

"Yep."

"You don't sound overly enthusiastic," said Hattie.

"I'm not."

"Come now, medieval adultery has its fascinations."

"Adultery!" Sarah shrieked. Hattie and Shirley exchanged quick glances. "What do you mean, adultery?"

"Lancelot and Guinevere, of course," Hattie said.

"Are you kidding me?" Sarah was stunned.

"Well, darling," Aunt Hattie responded slowly, "what do you think they were doing?"

"Well, they sort of were very attracted to each other, but, gosh, I don't think—" Sarah felt awash in confusion. "I don't think . . ." She paused.

Shirley was looking at her daughter helplessly. She began chewing on her Hi-Liter marker.

"Well, I don't think they actually—you know—did it," Sarah resumed.

Shirley and Hattie nodded silently.

"It's a heck of a punishment, to have to spend the rest of your days in a convent for just winking and blushing," Hattie said.

"Well, maybe they kissed and stuff," Sarah added.

"Shirley, have you done the birds and the bees bit with Sarah?"

"Don't make fun of me!" Sarah jumped up in fury and stood over her aunt and mother. She felt like a tremulous column of blood, tears, and anger. Sometimes she really did hate Aunt Hattie. Hattie had made fun of her. Mocked her. " 'Mockery is the fume of little hearts'!" Hattie's and Shirley's jaws dropped.

"I wasn't mocking you, darling," Hattie said. "I merely wanted to suggest that there might have been something physical going on between Guinevere and Lancelot."

"Miss Hoffritz said their love was imperfect."

"You mean Miss Hoffritz has taught all of *Idylls of the King* without ever mentioning adultery?" Hattie asked, her voice drenched in wonder.

"Yes!" Sarah hissed. "You think Stuart Hall should give us a rebate on our tuition?"

As soon as she had shut her bedroom door, Sarah thought of a million good things she should have said to Aunt Hattie about adultery, Lancelot, Arthur, and Guinevere. After all, one can be unfaithful in mind, not just body, and that obviously was what had been happening up there where the air was so fine and the light so pure. In the golden realm of Camelot, to be faithless in mind was equivalent to being faithless in body elsewhere, say in Indianapolis, she was sure. And she was mad. Birds and bees! She had a sudden urge to call Marla. Hattie and her mom were still in her mom's bedroom. She would go into the den and use that phone.

The phone rang twice.

"Hello." It was a male voice.

"Is Marla there?"

"May I ask who's calling?"

The nerve! "It's her sister. Any objections?"

"No, no." He laughed easily. "Just a minute. I'll get her." He spoke with a slight accent. Where could he have gone to get her? Marla's apartment was minuscule.

"Hello, Sarah, what's up?"

"Who's the foreigner?"

"A friend from school."

"And what took you so long?"

"I was in the bathroom."

"You were!" He would practically have to be in the bathroom with her in that shoe-box apartment. How embarrassing!

"What did you call about?"

"Well——" She had intended to talk to Marla about Guinevere, Lancelot, and medieval adultery, but somehow she had lost her enthusiasm for the subject. What if Marla laughed at her, too? "When do you get home for Christmas?"

"The nineteenth. You should see how pretty it is here in New York. They really go all out with the decorations. And on Park Avenue they have all these potted Christmas trees with tiny twinkly lights."

"Oooh! It sounds beautiful. I wish we could have a Christmas tree."

"You know, Sarah, I was thinking the same thing myself. It doesn't have to be that religious. Maybe we could talk Mom and Dad into getting one, just a small one, and some of those little lights. You know, we could just put on some nondenominational ornaments like candy canes and snowmen. Christmas is really sort of like a national holiday."

"That's a great phrase—national holiday. And I like nondenominational ornaments, too. I'll go to work on them tonight."

"Great! Gosh, I miss you, Sarah."

"I miss you, Marla. Everything is so boring here. Elaine is all wrapped up in her boyfriend. He's a real creep, and he picks his nose. I'm so sick of pageant rehearsal, and every week it seems they make up a new set of rules."

"Well, that's just high school, Sarah. Things get better, believe me. You get more control. You get more power over things."

Power was important. No wonder Mom liked reading about corporate power and Marla liked living on her own in New York and she herself hated being a shepherd.

141

"By the way, Marla, not to change the subject, but did you read *Idylls of the King*?"

"Sure."

"Well, tell me something. Do you think Guinevere and Lancelot really did it?"

"You mean went to bed together?" Marla asked.

"Yeah," Sarah said uneasily.

"Well, of course," Marla laughed.


That laugh of Marla's, so merry, so easy, seemed to ring in Sarah's ears all evening. It seemed to Sarah that sex had become some sort of joke and that, although she understood, she simply did not find the punch line as funny as the rest of the world did. There had to be something in-between the raucous merriment of Hattie and Marla and the detached golden reveries of Miss Hoffritz.

She was in the midst of her third and last proof of a geometric theorem when the phone rang.

"It's for you," her mother called. "It's Elaine."

"Okay. Coming." Sarah went into the den and picked up the phone. "Hi. . . . You're kidding. Ethan Johnson? Me? I don't really know him, but yeah I've seen him. He's cute! . . . Elaine, are you sure he's got the right Sarah Benjamin?" Sarah got up from the desk and carried the phone toward the doorway. There was a mirror in the hall, beside the coat closet. The phone line stretched just far enough to allow her to lean out to catch a reflection of her face. Ethan Johnson thinks I'm cute! she marveled. How could he? This is not only the face that did not launch a thousand ships, Sarah thought. It's a face with a zit on it and even when zitless has proved less than inspiring to countless Indianapolis boys. Who has never had a date to the Turkey Trot? Who has never been invited to a prom or any major social event? Sarah Benjamin, that's who!

Yes, there had been minor social interactions. Chickie Buckley, for example, had invited her to play miniature golf last July. But Chickie, as his name suggested, was not exactly a prince—not by a long shot. And to compound Chickie's inherent deficiencies, which were sufficient in themselves, Aunt Hattie had speculated at some length on what kind of parents would name a child "Chickie." She had speculated until Sarah's mother told her to shut up. Now, none other than Ethan Johnson had expressed interest in her. Not only that, but he'd told Elaine she was "cute."

Sarah tried to remember the last time she had thought she looked cute, or even vaguely presentable from the point of view of the opposite sex. She had looked okay at Yom Kippur services. Aunt Hattie had given her a neat-looking gray dress from Saks Fifth Avenue in New York. She had not had any pimples that week. Leave it to her face to clear up for the High Holy Days and break out for a dance! Besides, how cute can you look in a religious situation? She hated going to temple. Her mother always said she had a very sour look on her face during services. It was a moot point anyway. The chances of Ethan Johnson's being at Yom Kippur services at the Indianapolis Hebrew Congregation were nil.

"So Elaine, are you serious? He's going to invite me to the Christmas dance at the Indianapolis Athletic Club? You're kidding. . . . Oh gads! I don't know what to do. . . . Are you sure? You know, this could be a very cruel joke. I mean, like. . . . When's he going to call? Tonight? Tomorrow? . . . Are you going? What are you going to wear? Oh gads! I don't have anything. . . . Gee! Maybe. . . . Oh, Elaine, I'm so excited!"

"Dinner!" Shirley Benjamin looked into the den. "What's happening?" she asked as she saw Sarah dancing about with the phone.

"I'll tell you in a minute. Elaine, okay, listen, I'm going to keep

143

the lines clear. I'll call you back the minute I hear from him. . . .
Okay, bye-bye."

"Dad!" Sarah yelled, racing into the dining room. "Are you
on call tonight?"

"No, why?"

"Oh goodie! We have to keep the phones clear."

"Sarah, light meat or dark meat and why must the phones be
clear?" Shirley asked as she spooned green beans onto a plate.

"Yes, do tell," said Hattie—slyly, Sarah thought. She knows.
Sarah sat down warily. She knows even before Mom and Dad. It
wasn't just that Hattie was intuitive. She was invasive with her
knowledge.

"Dark." Sarah paused. "A guy might call me."

"Sarah, that's wonderful," Shirley exclaimed. The serving fork
froze in the air.

Sarah did wish her mother would not respond with such
jubilant alarm. Granted, her social life had been less than overwhelming since she had entered high school, but her mother's ec-
stasy, Sarah felt, was really too much.

"W-w-what guy?" Shirley stammered.

"Who? Who?" Alf asked.

"Ethan Johnson."

"Ethan! Ethan Johnson!" trilled Aunt Hattie. "What a divine
name—Ethan Allen, Ethan Frome, Ethan. Did he come over on
the Mayflower?"

"Oh, Hattie!" Shirley waved the serving fork in admonition.
"You and your white Anglo-Saxon Protestant fantasies."

"Nonsense, Shirley, I'm just a sucker for names. You have to
admit that Ethan Johnson is a marvelous name."

"Stop with the name already!" Alf nearly shouted. "Who is
he?"

"He goes to Park," Sarah replied.

"Park? What's Park?" Hattie asked.

"The boys' school. Stuart Hall's counterpart."

"Oh. Okay, continue, dear. I just have to have the libretto, you understand, to follow all this. How exciting! A marvelous boy with a divine name who goes to Park. Already we know he's monied."

"Hattie!" Alf exploded. "Would you let Sarah tell it. Sarah," he said, turning to her, "you do not have to include his stock portfolio, genealogy, or whatever. Just tell us in the lingo of the day is he cute, neat, a slob, moronic."

"Cute and neat," Sarah said.

"See?" Alf turned and smiled smugly at Hattie and Shirley. "I know what's important."

"Ah! Always the surgeon, Alfie! A few quick strokes through the subcutaneous layers to the true meat of the matter," Hattie said.

They were just finishing dinner when the phone rang. Sarah swallowed the yelp that was about to spring from her throat and slammed down the two hundred calories that perched on her fork in the form of a bite of cheesecake. She jumped up and ran to the kitchen phone.

"Hello." She could feel six ears in the dining room straining toward the kitchen. "What?" There was a muffled, snuffly voice on the other end. "Oh. . . . Yeah, sure. I'll get him." Sarah walked back into the dining room.

"Well?" Shirley said, and everybody looked at her.

"It's a rhino."

"A rhino?" Hattie asked.

"Rhinoplasty—nose-job patient," Shirley offered.

"Who is it?" Alf asked.

"A Mrs. Morris. She's calling from the hospital and she wants you to repack her nose because she's afraid some all-thumbs intern will wreck your 'masterpiece,' as she put it."

"Oh, for Lord's sake!" Alf flung his napkin down on the table.

"I'll tell you, if my one date of the year is wrecked by a nose job I'm going to have a fit."

"Don't worry, kiddo." Alf patted her shoulder.

"Just tell her your other masterpiece is waiting for a phone call, please!" Sarah called after her dad.

Shirley leaned over. "Don't worry, honey. He'll be quick. He'll probably have to call the chief resident. That will only take a second!" Shirley looked at Hattie. "I think he has two or three hysterical rhinos a week."

"Well, they're good for, what, three or four thousand dollars a week, aren't they?"

"I suppose." Shirley stood up and began to clear the table. "Just think of it that way, Sarah. Your road to a college education is being paved by bent noses your father straightens out."

"Mmm," replied Sarah.

"All clear," Alf said, smiling broadly as he came back into the dining room. "She's my only packed rhino tonight, so fear not."

The call came an hour later, in the middle of a Latin translation about Gaius Cornelius traveling from Baiae to Rome. It was a passage out of Seneca's *Epistolae Morales*. Sarah raced across the hall into her parents' bedroom and slammed the door. It was as if there were three voices on the phone—Ethan's, Sarah's, and this other Sarah's that seemed to whisper parenthetically between the other two.

ETHAN: Hi, this is Ethan Johnson, Sarah. How are you doing?

SARAH: Oh fine. How are you?

(SARAH): (Fine except for a mild case of hysteria.)

ETHAN: What I was calling about was, uh . . .

146

(SARAH):  (I know what you're calling about. Ho-ho-ho.
        Do try to be cool, Sarah!)

ETHAN:  Well, I was wondering if maybe you'd like to go
        to the Christmas dance at the Indianapolis Athletic
        Club with me.

(SARAH):  (Don't be silly. I'm all booked up.)

SARAH:  Gee yes. That sounds nice. When is it?

ETHAN:  December 21.

SARAH:  Oh sure. I'm free.

(SARAH):  (Of course you're free, you idiot. What else
        would you be doing? Repacking a hysterical rhino
        for your dad?)

ETHAN:  Uh, do you by any chance know what color dress
        you might be wearing?

SARAH:  Why?

(SARAH):  (Why! You idiot! How could you have said such
        a stupid thing. *Why?* Terminal embarrassment. He'll
        think you've never been anywhere. You retard!)

ETHAN:  Well, I thought I might get you a corsage.

SARAH:  Oh yeah.

(SARAH):  (What color? I don't have a dress. Flesh col-
        ored? Borrow Marla's? . . . What color would ev-
        erything go with? White? Oh, I'll look like a bride.
        Red? Never. Green? All those Christmas colors.
        How about tinsel? . . .)

SARAH:  Bluish.

ETHAN:  Bluish?

(SARAH):  (Yeah, rhymes with Jewish. Oh, you're a real
        card, Sarah. Why don't you just shut up.)

The conversation finished quickly.

"Ta*dah!*" Grinning, Sarah came into the den. Her dad got up and turned down the volume on the TV. "Miracles will never cease. I don't believe it. You actually shut Perry Mason up." Sarah glanced at the set and watched as a grim-faced Raymond Burr soundlessly approached the jury box, nodding and jabbing the air with his finger.

"So?" Shirley asked. "Come on, what happened?"

"Is he as divine as his name suggests?" Aunt Hattie asked.

"Oh yes, Aunt Hattie. I could tell from his voice that he was wearing a little pilgrim hat, you know you can always tell these things. Besides, he said the Mayflower was a real blast and he's happy to be here in Indianapolis practicing religious tolerance."

"*Sarah!*" Her mother screamed. "Did he invite you or not?"

"Of course he invited me. But do me a favor—don't act too excited about it."

"Why not? It's a very exciting event," Alf offered.

And then, in one of those unexpected flashes of true insight she occasionally exhibited, Aunt Hattie spoke. "It is not an event, Alf and Shirley. I know exactly what Sarah means. This should be treated as a normal occurrence in the life of an attractive adolescent girl like Sarah. Let's not make too big a deal out of it." Hattie got up and walked across the carpet in her little dragon slippers. "He really should go on a diet," she said, nodding at the television. "Without that sonorous voice he's just a tub of lard." She turned up the volume.

Well, bless her one-eyed vision, Sarah thought as she returned to Gaius Cornelius on the road from Baiae to Rome. But first she detoured into her parents' bedroom to call Elaine.

# Chapter Nineteen

"Now, girls, nothing monumental," Alf said as they walked through the rows of trees propped against fencing.

They had driven directly from the airport to a Christmas-tree lot near the corner of Route 421 and Kessler Boulevard.

"No, no!" said Marla excitedly. "Just a small, discreet tree appropriate for a reformed Jewish family."

Sarah was surveying another row. "Oooh, look at this one! Isn't it cute." She pulled a short, squat, bushy one away from the fence.

"Oh, I'm not sure," said Marla. "I was thinking more in terms of lean and elegant."

"Oh, but this one has personality," Sarah said.

"Personality?" Alf said, looking at Shirley as he wrapped his muffler higher on his chin and pulled down his hat.

"Alf, are you trying to hide, dear? If you pull that muffler any higher or that cap any lower you'll be invisible. Are you nervous about this?"

"I am not hiding, Shirley. I am not nervous in the least. I think the girls are right. It is simply a national holiday. There will be nondenominational ornaments on our tree."

"And," Sarah added, "cookie angels—right? Those are still included?"

"We get to have cookie angels?" Marla asked excitedly.

"Yes. As long as you can eat an angel it's not real, Dad says."

"I said that?" Alf peered out between his muffler and cap.

"Well, something like it. And they're going to have chocolate hair, Marla. No more blonde angels—at least not on our tree."

"That's probably why I said you could have the angels," Alf said. "Gives a little ethnic variation to the notion."

"Remember the Angel Perception Analysis!"

"Can we have entirely chocolate angels?" Marla asked.

"Of course. I've got the dough all made up. All of this is a result of my landmark study."

"Did Martin Luther King believe in black angels? I forget."

"Of course. He believed in all kinds of angels. All colors— kind of a rainbow."

"Oooh! That's beautiful," Marla said. "We could make all kinds of different-colored frostings."

Which was just what they did. It was an exquisitely happy evening. Marla and Sarah cut little angels with a template Sarah had made. Shirley helped them mix up a rainbow variety of frosting glazes, which sat in little teacups ready to be painted on the freshly baked cookies, and Alf ate any fractured angels, ones with broken wings and parts beyond repair. In those cases deemed salvageable by the girls or Shirley, he was called upon to perform plastic surgery and reattachment procedures using thickened frosting. On the tape recorder was a tape Lieba had sent Sarah as a Hanukkah present. In her first postbaby performance, she had brought down the house with the great C Major fugue of Bach for solo violin. Although her first really big New York appearance was some time off, word of this single performance had spread rapidly and Lieba had been signed by Angel Records for an album.

"How is Lieba, Marla?" Shirley asked.

"Great. Liberty is incredibly cute, very fat. Looks just like Shlomo. They're dying for Sarah to come and visit."

"Oh, I wish I could go, Mom. I *am* the godmother. Lieba said so. I should go and do some godmotherly thing."

"Like what?" Marla said.

"We sent him a darling little playsuit for Hanukkah," Shirley said.

"You sent him that, Mom. I sent Liberty a space helmet."

"A space helmet?" Marla said, looking up from the chocolate hair she was piping onto an angel cookie with a pastry tube. "What in heaven's name does little Liberty Yossel Bell Rabinowitz need with a space helmet?"

"Little kids hate getting clothes for presents," Sarah said emphatically. "They want toys. I remember when I was a kid. It was always such a disappointment to open the box and see that neatly arranged tissue paper around some cutesy outfit. Believe me, this space helmet will take him a lot farther than some little terry-cloth stretch suit."

"She's probably right," Shirley said.

"Should I get you a space helmet for your next birthday, Sarah?" Alf said. "Pass me that broken wing. Mmmm. These are scrumptious."

"No, I'm *into* the clothes phase of my development now. Speaking of which, Marla has to go with me tomorrow to see The Dress."

"This is The Dress for The Dance with The Ethan, I take it?"

"Right. There are actually two dresses they are holding for me at Ayre's. One is—"

"Bluish," Shirley chimed in, smiling.

"Bluish?" Marla asked.

"It's a long story," Sarah said. "The other one is pink."

"Sarah, did you tell Marla about going shopping with Aunt Hattie?"

Marla rolled her eyes. "I can't imagine anything worse."

"Yes you can," Sarah said, licking up an errant squirt of chocolate hair from the counter.

"What?" Marla asked.

"Getting run over by a truck."

"It was a riot," Shirley said.

"You might have thought it was funny, Mother. I did not."

"No, Marla, you should have seen this," Shirley said. "Hattie sashays into the Sunvale Shop in Broad Ripple—you know, where everybody gets prom dresses and graduation stuff, bridesmaids' outfits—and she's wearing that mocha mink jacket of hers."

"Isn't that disgusting?" Sarah said, biting the head off a half-burnt angel. "Can you imagine calling a mink 'mocha'? Poor animal! I'm never going to wear fur coats, let alone insult them with an adjective like that."

"Well, that's what Hattie calls it. Anyway, we're in the shop," Shirley continued, "and there are all those girls from that big Swanson wedding trying on these huge bouffant taffeta dresses. Hattie turns around and says, 'What is this? A Scarlett O'Hara dress-alike contest?' And then she says—oh, this is so funny." Shirley began to giggle. Soon she was laughing so hard that she had to sit down. "She says . . ." Shirley started, but again burst out laughing. She wiped her eyes. "She whispered to me, 'You know, virginity is fine. But I've never liked it as a clothing concept!' "

"Oh no!" Marla moaned. "Poor Sarah!"

"Exactly." Sarah nodded. "And she didn't whisper it either. It reverberated throughout the store. It was mortifying. Can you imagine having to go shopping with that nut? And when we get to Ayre's, what does she do? You won't believe it, Marla. You tell her, Mom."

"Yes, that was a bit much," Shirley said, still wiping tears of laughter from her face.

"Oh, the nightgown thing," Alf said.

"Nightgown?" Marla asked.

"You'd better believe it," Sarah said. "I'm trying on the bluish thing. It's really pretty and it has these silvery little figures all over it."

"It is pretty, Marla," Shirley added.

"Anyway, The Hat comes in with, wouldn't you know, her favorite color—a café au lait satin nightgown with these fake ostrich feathers attached. Then, in this shy little voice, because she knows I'll probably punch her in her good eye, she says, 'Sarah, dear heart.' " Squinting one eye shut, Sarah slipped into a perfect imitation of Hattie. " 'Sarah, darling, I just want to offer this little suggestion—a kind of creative alternative to your little bluish tulle number with those silver measles.' Can you believe it? She wanted me to wear this thing, this nightgown. Forget the fact that I'd look like a toad in it, forget the fact that I would die of the cold in it, be frozen stiff: It was absolutely impossible to wear a bra under it. Of course, according to The Hat, none of the New York fashion models ever wear bras. Is that true, Marla?"

"I never checked."

"Well, can you imagine me going to the Christmas dance at the Indianapolis Athletic Club without a bra? I mean, even though I am not particularly well endowed?"

"No, I can't."

"Hattie had visions of Jean Harlow," Shirley offered.

"Who's Jean Harlow?"

"Was," Alf and Shirley said in unison.

"I'm sure I don't look a thing like her."

"You don't," Marla said.

"What did she look like anyway?"

"Sort of like Marilyn Monroe," Shirley said. "A little slinkier and sleeker. Very platinum hair. And she wore satiny gowns."

153

"Oh!" said Sarah. "I understand perfectly why Hattie imme-diately thought of me and that nightgown. I mean, people stop me all the time downtown: 'Are you Jean Harlow? Oh gee, I was certain you were. You sure are a dead ringer for her.' Gads! I should really get a medal for endurance."

"Well, you're going to have a nice long respite from Aunt Hattie."

"How long is she gone for?"

"A couple of months. Vronsky's in London, then Paris. Next she has to go out West. Shlomo's doing a lot in California. Then Vronsky's got an extended engagement in Stuttgart, and I think Hattie will stay in his apartment in New York because it coincides with a lot of Lieba's East Coast stuff."

"She's got to find Lieba and Shlomo a place to live other than hers," Marla said.

"It's very hard to find those places. Anyhow, she's hardly here at all these days. She's in and out. No problem."

"Speak for yourself!" Sarah said.

"Now, Sarah, I know she can be irritating."

"Irritating!" squealed Sarah in mock surprise. "Aunt Hattie, irritating? Never! Whatever gave you that idea. Just because she has a word of advice on everything I do, an opinion on everything under the sun, likes only the colors mocha, crème de ca-ca, and café au lait, and tries to paint everything including me those colors, why would you ever imagine I would find her irritating?"

"Let's get these angels onto the tree," Marla said.

They had settled on the short, bushy tree. It did not appear all that short, however, in the living room. It was about as tall as Sarah. First the girls strung tiny white bulbs just like the Park Avenue lights Marla had described. Then they began to hang the frosted angels. Shirley and Alf settled on the couch, Alf reading a newspaper, Shirley a finance text. The preceding day Sarah had made snowman cookies and bought two boxes of candy canes and a box of clear glass balls.

Shirley looked over her reading glasses at the tree. "It looks lovely, girls. Those lights reflect beautifully in the glass, and the frosting on the angels looks so shimmery. This was a very nice idea."

"Maybe we should officially celebrate Marla's homecoming," Alf said. "I've got a bottle of champagne in the basement refrigerator."

"Oh, how festive!" Shirley said.

"Let me put on some really festive music," Marla added.

In less than five minutes Alf was removing the cork. As he poured the champagne Marla and Sarah hung the last ornaments. Then he handed out the glasses. "Well, kiddos—l'chaim," he said, lifting his glass.

"To life!" echoed Shirley.

The Christmas tree twinkled. The air seemed colored by the brilliant music, a rain of silvery sounds as the Cleveland Orchestra played Handel's *Water Music*. Sarah sipped small amounts of champagne and felt tiny explosions of bubbles on the underside of her nose. She saw the angels quiver on the tree as the sounds of the *Water Music* wrapped around them. She squinted her eyes during a crescendo and saw a shimmering rainbow of colors. This was perfect. Outside it was a cold and starless night; yet inside there was this sensation of stars and constellations, an entire galaxy under one roof. It was a world, a universe, just four people in it, and for that one night it was all Sarah thought she'd ever need.

# Chapter Twenty

Sarah and Ethan had not double-dated, as she had hoped they would, with Elaine and Stephen. And although Ethan was indeed cute and very nice and the dance was lovely, Sarah had never really even begun to feel at ease. She could not quite figure out why. It was not as if there were long, awkward lulls; they had found plenty to talk about. Maybe if Ethan had been a smidge less handsome she would have felt better. But the entire evening she had this lurking feeling that his asking her was some sort of mistake, as if he had confused her with someone else . . . Lacey Denton, perhaps!

She had settled, with Marla's advice, on the bluish dress. Elaine said she looked gorgeous in it. She had gone to her mom's hairdresser, Mr. Ben—or Gentle Ben, as she and Marla called him. He had fixed her hair to look just like the model's on the cover of the *Mademoiselle* magazine she had brought. It was very straight, just brushing her shoulders, and on either side of her center part a skinny little braid looped back, fastened at the back of her head with a pretty clip. Marla had done her eye makeup. She did not have one single zit. This was as good as she was ever going to look. She could tell when she came to the door that Ethan thought she looked pretty good, too. He was not disappointed. It had not been a mistake. All evening, she kept reminding herself of the way he had looked at her when she opened the door.

Then why the unease? she thought as they were dancing. Was she nervous about his physical closeness? She could tell that he shaved—and not just peach fuzz. It was not totally dull to have one's cheek, specifically her cheek, brushed by his cheek, which had this roughness. It wasn't just that he was cute. He was also "cool." That was it! Cool—the adjective that suffused everybody's talk and attitudes; cool—the cardinal virtue celebrated by all, possessed by few. That's so cool. He's so cool. She's so cool. What a cool idea. The very word implied a distance, a kind of wall, between "the cool" and those who were not. The opposite of cool was not necessarily uncool. It was not necessarily a negative condition at all. It was simply what the rest of the world was.

Sarah would have felt so much better if Ethan had been just plain handsome. Because, she reflected, as they danced through a red spotlight that turned her bluish dress purple, when you're cool you're not only distant, which is really a matter of style. You are also sort of uninvolved. And because you're uninvolved, you're never in any kind of danger. Well, she didn't really mean physical danger. It was just that you were not vulnerable. Being constantly vulnerable wasn't a desirable condition, of course; but perhaps it made one more—more complicated. That was it! Ethan seemed so simplified. And at that moment as they whirled to the music, Sarah realized for the first time ever that she missed The Hat. The Hat was the most complicated person Sarah knew. Right there in the middle of the red spotlight, she realized that Aunt Hattie must in some very secret, complicated way be vulnerable. Sarah's eyes opened wide to this profound shock.

After the dance, instead of driving straight to Sarah's, they had gone to the house of Jeff Edwards (one of Ethan's cool friends), where his very nice but uncool mother and father had made a delicious late-night breakfast for them. Sarah sat at a long kitchen counter with Ethan and some other kids while Mr. Edwards talked to them and Mrs. Edwards slid trays of toasted bagels and cream cheese in their direction. Sarah knew the family was not Jewish, so how had they stumbled across bagels? There was hardly a gentile west of New Jersey, she figured, who knew what bagels were, let alone bought them. This was equivalent to an Eskimo having a stash of spaghetti sauce or a Bedouin munching wontons. It was uncool but complicated, which Sarah felt went to show that coolness was not in the genes. Mr. and Mrs. Edwards's conversation was sort of nice, too. They were remembering when they had dated, or "courted," as Mr. Edwards had said, and had gone for summer dances at an outdoor place called Stars-on-the-River, which was near the White River. "Before the river smelled," Mr. Edwards said, "and when the summer skies were always clear."

Sarah wouldn't have minded staying longer at the Edwardses'. She was actually enjoying the breakfast more than she had the dance, but she could tell that Ethan was not. He kept rolling his eyes at Mr. Edwards's remarks and when he couldn't catch Sarah with a rolling eye he tried to catch one of his cool friends, including Jeff. Sarah guessed that Jeff Edwards would most likely chew his parents out after the guests left. It would be terminally embarrassing to a cool person to have parents who served bagels and talked about summer dances that they'd attended a quarter of a century ago.

It was bitterly cold when Ethan pulled the car over to the side of a small road near the Kessler Boulevard bridge. I don't believe this is happening to me, Sarah thought. How am I going to tell him I don't want to park? Ethan switched off the ignition. Panic rose in Sarah's throat. Oh Lord, he's going to want to make out.

"I brought a little something to warm us up." He spoke in a low, ultracool voice as he reached into the glove compartment and took out a small bottle.

Sarah's "oh" was barely audible. He took off the cap. "Want some?" he offered.

"No, thank you." "Thank you" sounded nicer than just "thanks." She didn't want to sound abrupt. She especially didn't want to anger Ethan Johnson. But she had to be able to say no, somehow, some way. Slow dancing close in red spotlights was one thing. Face it, she had thought about kissing him. Her mind had not stopped at the feel of peach fuzz and bristles. But now she felt crushed in the darkness of the front seat of this car on a cold winter night with a bottle of liquor, by a frozen river—with this stranger and no time to wonder.

Ethan put his arm around her and tugged at her so that she sank back against him. This was not intolerable. If she could just sort of lean against him and keep it at that it would be okay.

"That was interesting, what Mr. Edwards said about that dance place, wasn't it?"

"Not particularly."

Oh Lord! Sarah thought. Super cool. Couldn't he have just said "yeah" without conviction? After all, she had made an effort to avoid sounding abrupt. Sarah persisted. "The river really has gotten scummy in the last few years. Margery Webber did a project on the pollution this fall." Sarah's voice began to dwindle. She could feel Ethan's hand creeping inside her coat. Desperately she wondered how to say no without offending him. "Margery said that you shouldn't eat any of the fish from the river, and . . ."

Sarah would never know which had come first, the hand or the word, but suddenly she felt his finger on her nipple and heard *nigger* on his lips: "Only niggers fish down there anyway." Her blood froze.

As she removed his hand her thoughts came with astounding swiftness and clarity. Her voice was creamily smooth. It was a voice that sounded totally strange, as if some other person were speaking. "Ethan . . ." The name slid out like a flat, broad, cooked noodle.

159

There was no hint of agitation in her tone. "I'm awfully cold." She smiled sweetly. He wouldn't know what she was doing until it was too late. "It's my feet." He opened his eyes a little wider as if that would help him comprehend what she was saying. He might have expected rejection, but not a comment on the coldness of her feet. "Could I borrow your socks?" She paused and smiled intimately. "I like to be comfortable, you know." Her heart had begun to pound wildly in her chest. She felt that anyone within a hundred feet could have heard it.

"Oh sure," Ethan said, and began to take off his shoes. "I suppose your boots don't do much over just nylons and high heels."

He had fallen for it. There was something slightly insinuating in his voice when he said the word *nylons*. He handed her the socks. She had removed her boots and high-heeled shoes. She put on the socks, slipped on her boots, and tucked her shoes under one arm. Her hand was on the door.

"Well, so long," she said, and opened the door.

"So *what?*" Ethan said, and probably for the first time in his cool life he looked totally confused. "You mad about me feeling you up?" She was about to say that was minor in comparison to his racial slur, but when she thought of her size thirty triple-A bra she realized that she might start laughing or perhaps crying if she said *minor*. "That and what you said about the people who fish in the river."

"You-mean niggers?"

"Yes, and don't use that word around me ever again!"

"Are you part colored or something?"

"No, you idiot, I'm white and I'm Jewish. Or would you say I'm a 'kike'?"

"Sarah, where are you going?"

"Home."

160

"You walking?"

"It's less than a mile."

"But Sarah, you can't. Look, I'm really sorry. I'll take you home. It wouldn't be right. I'm responsible."

Sarah leaned in through the open door. "Listen, you creep, don't kid yourself. Nobody can be responsible and be a bigot at the same time. And I don't share anything with jerks like you. Not cars, not rides, nothing."

"You can't walk all that way on a night like this!" Ethan protested.

"I've done it before and I'll do it again and you'd better not follow me."

"My socks!" Ethan said weakly.

"Don't worry, you'll get them back." Sarah smiled. A few flakes of snow had started to fall. "I'll have my dad drop them off, or better yet, my Aunt Hattie."

Sarah turned away. Within a minute she was on the bridge. Had it been only eleven months ago that she and Elaine and Lieba had walked this same route? Had they pressed the snow with prints of angels on this very same bridge? She thought now of niggers and nipples, starless skies and blank heavens, kikes and catfish. As she neared the end of the bridge her own tears thawed and she knew that she was making this journey through a night without prayer. It was hard to believe that the earth could be a speck of light in another's vision.

# Chapter Twenty-one

$\mathcal{S}$he had stood that evening in the kitchen in her bluish dress and Ethan Johnson's socks, her baby's-breath-and-sweetheart-rose corsage limp on the bodice of her dress. Her mother and father and Marla had stared mutely at her as she told them between gulps and sobs the brief, disastrous tale. She had not been too graphic. She had left out the part about the nipple. But they got the gist of the experience: thwarted sex, bigotry, and booze. Her father had said she had done the right thing. He could become maniacal at the thought of drinking and driving. That was what he chose to focus on. Her mother and Marla's focus seemed to be the sweetheart corsage. The roses were crushed and faded and hung like little dead birds at her shoulder. Shirley just stared and stared at the corsage until finally Sarah unpinned it and walked over to the sink. She held it up. "Is this like banana peels? Will it foul up the disposal?"

"No," Shirley said softly. "Grind it up."

Much later, just before dawn, Sarah crawled into bed with Marla and told her about the nipple and cried and cried while Marla held her tight.

"Do I have an idea for you, Sarah Benjamin!" That was what Alf Benjamin had said one evening three weeks after the disastrous Christmas dance as he slapped his hands together in strained gaiety.

Sarah had not "bounced back" as she was supposed to have done. A lot of families, well-to-do middle-class families, would have taken their depressed daughter to a psychiatrist, but Sarah knew that this would not be Alf's hand-slapping inspiration. She knew she was safe from psychiatry because of the plastic surgeon's bias against it: Having spent twenty-five years piecing together torn ears and faces blown apart by .38-caliber bullets, for him the value of psychiatry as a healing art ranked somewhere between consulting a Ouija board and gargling with saltwater.

So when Sarah did not "bounce back," instead of taking her to a shrink they took her to Disneyland. That was Alf's wonderful idea.

"Disneyland?" Sarah said vaguely.

"Yeah," replied Alf. "There's a convention for plastic surgeons out there."

"At Disneyland? What are they doing, a nose job for Mickey Mouse?"

"Oh, Sarah!" Shirley and Alf hooted in unison. They laughed just a little too hard at her joke, Sarah thought. "We were going to spend a few days out there anyway, going to the desert. And we think a little trip might be, well . . ." Alf hesitated.

"Fun," Shirley added quickly. "You deserve some fun."

Somehow it didn't sound right. One didn't "deserve" fun. One simply had it. And in Sarah's case, if she did deserve it, it was only because her social life was such a colossal failure.

"Come on, Sarah, it'll be better than staying here with Mrs. Nicholson."

Alf's secretary often stayed with Sarah when her parents had to go away. "Well . . ." Sarah said grudgingly. She supposed they were right. The Hat was still in Europe. Staying home with Mrs. Nicholson would definitely not be "fun." But somehow Disneyland was not the New Frontier she and Marla had envisioned on election night two years before.

Two weeks later, Sarah did find herself traveling down the perilous waters of the "Amazon" on a "jungle cruise" in Adventureland. Their jungle guide had the most wretched sense of humor Sarah had ever encountered.

"Welcome aboard, ladies and gentlemen. You, too, Crocodile Bait," he added, looking at a chubby baby sitting on its mother's lap. "The name of our boat is *Python Pol*. Now, folks, as we leave, wave good-bye to the people on shore. It will probably be the last time you see them. Yes sirree, the cruise of no return."

"This guy's a real card," Shirley whispered.

The guide blathered on. "The natives are restless—uh-oh! Get down in the boat, folks." A tribe of feather-garbed animatronic natives with spears did a war dance on the banks just a few feet from where the hippos had surfaced and "shown their pearly whites." "Around the next bend, folks, the neighborhood head shrinker. . . . A real bargain, ladies and gentlemen, he'll trade you two of his for one of yours. . . . Ah, we're approaching the pool of frolicking Indian elephants. Don't worry, ladies, they keep their trunks on!" Alf laughed a little too hard at this joke, and Shirley elbowed him in the ribs.

Sarah tried to look cheerful. After all, wasn't this better than sitting in English class listening to Miss Hoffritz get weepy over "Lake Isle of Innisfree"? Mechanical crocodiles in 75-degree temperatures really were nicer than 15-degree temperatures and endless days at Stuart Hall. Her parents had bought her scads of new clothes at Robinson's in Beverly Hills. She was wearing a brand-new madras skirt with sewn-down pleats, her Villager blouse, and squeaking new Weejuns. But why was she almost ready to cry?

The Ethan Johnson disaster had been weeks ago, so it couldn't be just that. Here her parents had rearranged their plans to include her. The problem was that she was so confused. Was this life, traveling through a plastic kingdom, or was Stuart Hall life, reading great poetry under the guidance of dried-up old maids? I should be grateful, Sarah thought. I have so much. I'm not just middle-class, I'm upper middle-class. I have a clothing allowance and still my parents buy most of my clothes. I have good grades. I have a canopy bed and eighteenth-century-reproduction wallpaper from the Metropolitan Museum in New York. My parents are happily married. I am the luckiest girl in the world.

The boat went around the bend, and the automated cannibals rejoiced over the tasty white hunter they had just captured for their pot. Miserable, Sarah fought back her tears. God might strike me dead for crying in Disneyland. I'm so rich. I'm so healthy. Just for this, I'll probably get leukemia and go directly to jail—do not pass go, do not collect two hundred dollars. No Fantasyland. No Frontierland. No Tomorrowland. You ungrateful, privileged wretch!

They had exited Adventureland, and her parents had stopped to buy some popcorn at the central plaza. Sarah had run just a few paces ahead, less than half a city block, to see a Disney Star of Stars parade: Mickey; Minnie; the seven dwarfs; Fess Parker, the original Davey Crockett; Ronald Reagan, the television host of "General Electric Theater"; Tiny Kline, the elderly-but-still-flying Tinker Bell; and assorted Mouseketeers. She followed in the tracks of Grumpy and Sneezy back to the popcorn cart, but her parents were nowhere in sight. Sarah was sure they had heard her when she told them she was going to see the parade for just a minute, and she had been gone for less than five. It was hard to imagine how she could have lost them so quickly. She waited patiently by the popcorn vendor. Five minutes passed, then ten. She was becoming nervous. She would take a turn around the plaza. There was no sign of them. They had said something about eating in Tomorrowland. She headed off in that direction. She scanned the customers at The

Lunching Pad. Twice she circled the Matterhorn, which had a sign up: SORRY FOR THE INCONVENIENCE—CLOSED FOR REFURBISHING.

She had a queasy feeling in her stomach. What if her parents had gone into the Matterhorn through some unguarded entrance and become lost or imprisoned? Marla's friend Grace Mobley had an uncle who had died falling off Mount Everest. But had anyone ever perished in a plastic chunk of the Swiss Alps? Was it really plastic? Sarah edged up close and touched the grainy surface. It did not feel like plastic. But it didn't feel like rock either. Cement-covered Styrofoam, perhaps? That was the problem in Disneyland—you couldn't tell what things really were. She would probably be kicked out for merely having the thought. After all, there were no problems in Disneyland. But it disturbed Sarah profoundly that too often she could not tell what was real and what was fake in this peculiar world that had been, as the guidebooks said, "imagineered" by storytellers, scientists, and moviemakers. Only the trash cans were what they seemed. There was no mistaking them.

One of Sarah's favorite attractions was the Swiss Family Robinson's tree house. It appeared just as it had in her book, without a detail lost: giant clamshells for water basins, net hammocks suspended between branches, the ship's wheel in the parlor, intricate systems of pulleys and ropes and ladders all lodged among the branches of the "tree." The leaves appeared so genuine that Sarah's mother had stopped to ask if real vines had been planted. "No, ma'am," the attendant replied. "What you see here are three hundred thousand vinyl leaves 'growing' on six tons of reinforced steel, one hundred and ten cubic yards of concrete. You are talking one hundred fifty tons of fun!" That had sort of finished it for Sarah. From there they had proceeded to the jungle cruise and bad jokes about babies and crocodile bait.

166

By now, forty-five minutes had passed. Still no sign of her parents. She looked at her souvenir guide. There was a Lost Children Center. Dare she turn herself in? Would they accept an almost-sixteen-year-old? What the heck. She was tired of waiting around by the popcorn vendor.

She headed down Main Street, turned left at a shop on the first corner, where she bought a postcard to send to Marla, went past the Buffeteria, and walked through a door marked with a red cross and a sign that said FIRST AID AND LOST CHILDREN. The room was cool and comfortable—tan carpeting, paneled walls, doctor's-office-style furniture. No pictures, no Mickeys or Minnies. This must be the place, Sarah thought, where people came not only when they were lost but also to recover from overdoses of cuteness.

"Not feeling well, dear?" A gray-haired lady in a nurse's uniform looked up from the desk where she was reading the *Los Angeles Times.* She wore trifocals.

"Not sick. Would you believe lost?"

"Don't worry about it. Sit down. I'm sure your parents will be here soon. Can I get you anything?"

"No, thanks, unless you have a pen. I think I'd like to write a postcard."

"Sure thing," the nurse said. "Help yourself." She indicated a tray on her desk with several pens on it. Sarah took one and got out the card she'd bought for Marla. It was a picture of Minnie and Mickey Mouse in a Model T in front of the Disneyland Town Hall.

Dear Marla,

Would you believe that I just turned myself in to the Lost Children Center at Disneyland? Mom and Dad lost me at a popcorn cart somewhere between Adventureland and the Matterhorn, which incidentally is closed for refurbishing. Don't worry about me. Nobody is ever really lost in Disneyland. If they are, the Disney engineers build them a set of audioanimatronic parents able to simulate human movements.

"Sarah!" The door opened, and in rushed Alf and Shirley.

"Oh Lord!" Alf said. "We thought we'd lost you for crocodile bait!"

The trifocaled nurse beamed through her split lenses at the happy reunion. She must do this twenty-five times a day, Sarah thought.

That night in the hotel Sarah finished the card to Marla.

I have been found at last! They are not animatronic. They are our real, original parents. Dad's beard grew even in Disneyland and Mom got a fever blister on her lip as usual from the sun.

She paused. The closing line should be standard, "and they all lived happily ever after." But Sarah simply could not bring herself to write that line even in this jokey card. So instead she signed off,

Molecules triumph over fantasy!
Love, Sarah

# PART IV

## NOVEMBER 1963

# Chapter Twenty-two

" 'And there were in the same country shepherds abiding in the field, keeping watch over their flock by night.' " Miss Crowninshield's voice became almost melodic in this part of the Gospel.

"Hey, guys," Phoebe Buxton whispered, "it's coming up. Our big dramatic moment!"

"Crooks ready?" Elaine asked.

"Check," replied Sarah.

"All systems go?" Phoebe asked.

"A-OK from the launch pad," Elaine answered.

"Hillary, start the countdown," Phoebe ordered.

"Ten."

" 'And, lo' "—the voice continued—" 'the angel of the Lord came upon them, and the glory of the Lord shone round about them—' "

"Nine," Hillary whispered.

" '—and they were sore afraid.' " Miss Crowninshield always drew this part out quite a bit with the help of some piano chords strategically punctuating the verses.

"Just think," Elaine said. "Emily Heath will miss quarterlies."

"That's the least of her problems," Phoebe whispered.

"Eight," whispered Hillary.

" 'And the angel said unto them . . .' " Crowninshield's voice grew stealthy.

"Why is Emily going to miss quarterly exams?" Sarah asked.

*"Why?"* The other three shepherds gasped in unison.

"Benjamin, where have you been?" Phoebe asked.

"Oh gosh!" Elaine whispered. "You were late this morning, weren't you?"

"Yeah," said Sarah. "What did I miss?"

"Everything!" Elaine answered.

" 'Fear not' "—the voice rose—" 'for, behold, I bring you good tidings of great joy . . .' "

"Not for Emily Heath," Phoebe muttered.

Miss Crowninshield had stopped in her narration to review some lighting cues with the stage crew.

"What are you talking about?" Sarah asked almost desperately.

"Emily Heath"—Elaine paused dramatically—"is pregnant."

"She's what?" gasped Sarah.

"Don't spit in my ear, Benjamin," said Phoebe. "If you have to spit, at least aim for my crook. You heard her. Emily is 'in the family way,' as the saying goes."

"Good grief!"

"You sound just like Charlie Brown," Phoebe whispered.

"But that's impossible!" Sarah exclaimed.

"Hardly," said Elaine. "Can you imagine having your pregnancy announced by Crowninshield?"

"She didn't!" Sarah was truly aghast.

"She did," Phoebe said.

"In morning announcements? Over the PA?" Sarah asked.

"No," Elaine said. "In a fit of extreme sensitivity she called a special morning assembly. I guess she felt it wasn't delicate to send news like this out over the airwaves."

"You mean you all came into the auditorium, right here, and Crowninshield stood up in front and told everybody about Emily?"

"Yep," Phoebe said.

"And guess what her parting words to us were?" Elaine said.

"How should I know?" Sarah asked.

"What are some of Crowninshield's favorite little expressions? Come on, think!"

Sarah thought. Crowninshield had a battery of little sayings that were designed to launch students on a life of industry and responsibility. What could she fetch out of her battery for this occasion? "Uh, 'a chain is only as strong as its weakest link.' "

"No."

" 'As the twig is bent so the tree is inclined'?"

"Nope. Get this," Elaine said. " 'A word to the wise is sufficient.' "

"Oh Lord!" Sarah muttered. "I still can't believe it about Emily. Yesterday Emily was sitting right next to me in American history making all sorts of insightful remarks about the Louisiana Purchase."

"A fat lot of good that's going to do her now," Elaine said.

Miss Crowninshield resumed the narration: " 'For unto you is born this day . . .' "

"Four," Hillary hissed in warning.

Sarah was absolutely dumbfounded. Emily Heath had, indeed, less than twenty-four hours before, been sitting next to her in history making organized, exquisitely written notes in her three-ring notebook. Emily was very meticulous. She always wrote down all the names of the principals under the heading *People*. There they had been: Talleyrand, Livingston, all of them. Under the heading *Details* were such facts as "828,000 square miles" and "80,000,000 francs." And the whole time she had been writing all of that a baby had been growing inside her!

" 'And this shall be a sign unto you; Ye shall find the babe wrapped in swaddling clothes, lying in a manger.' "

"Three." Hillary's voice was barely audible.

"But she's so quiet, kind of reserved," Sarah said. "I mean, I didn't even know she had a boyfriend."

"She's been seeing some guy from Culver Military Academy," Elaine said.

" 'And suddenly there was with the angel a multitude of the heavenly host praising God, and saying—' "

"Is she getting married to him?"

"Nope. His parents won't hear of it," Elaine said.

"Quit asking questions, Benjamin," Phoebe whispered. "We're almost ready to move."

"You're on my staff, Buxton," Elaine hissed.

"But listen," Sarah asked urgently. "What's she going to do?"

"She's being sent to a home for unwed mothers," Phoebe said.

"Oh no! Where?"

"Terre Haute."

"Terre Haute! Terre Haute, Indiana?"

"Terre Haute!" Hattie leaned forward toward Sarah and adjusted her eye patch slightly. "That's where John Dillinger was born, I think."

"Well, somebody else is going to be born there, too," Sarah said, sinking down onto the sofa. "Who's John Dillinger anyway?"

"A famous criminal," Shirley told her.

"Bank robber," Hattie added.

"Oh gosh, I hope this baby does better," Sarah said. She opened her Latin book and looked briefly at the stretch of Cicero she had to translate.

"I think it's tragic," Shirley said.

"Well, it would be more tragic if she had to marry the boy," Hattie said.

"Of course. But a home for unwed mothers in Terre Haute! And Emily was smart, didn't you say that, Sarah?"

"Not *was*. Is. You talk as if she's dead."

A yawn of silence seemed to engulf the den. There was not much to say. Sarah wondered exactly what Emily would do at this home for unwed mothers. Knit booties and read about the Louisiana Purchase? Emily was a wonderful math student. She'd probably do a few trigonometry problems every day just to keep herself sharp. But what for? Gads, it was depressing. She liked Emily. Emily was a senior and not stuck-up about it. Sarah had been in classes with her in the two areas where juniors and seniors could occasionally overlap, science and history. In their case it was American history and physics, and she had always been so helpful to Sarah. Physics! Sarah sat up straight on the sofa. Emily was her lab partner. How was Sarah going to survive the science fair without her?

"You know what, guys?" Sarah looked at her mother and aunt.

"What, dear?" Shirley asked.

"I'm going to almost flunk physics."

"Well, almost is better than actually flunking it." Alf Benjamin had come in from his office. "It's starting to sleet out there," he said. "It's cold. It's damp. I'm chilled to the proverbial marrow."

"How about a little toddy for the body," Hattie offered. "I'll fix it just like they do at the ski resorts—hot, with a good jolt of rum. Or would you prefer bourbon?"

"Rum will be fine. Okay, what's this about flunking physics?"

"Well," sighed Sarah, inverting her Latin text on top of her head and holding it in place.

"Why are you doing that with your book, dear?" Shirley asked.

"I like to wear Cicero as a hat. There's always the hope of providing a more direct page-to-brain route for the translation."

"Okay, okay," Alf said. "So what's the problem with physics?"

"Emily Heath is pregnant," Sarah answered, crushing Cicero more firmly onto her head.

Alf's eyes shifted quickly from Sarah to Shirley. He cleared his throat. "Did I miss something here? Emily Heath, whoever she is—"

"A senior."

"Okay, this senior is pregnant and you're flunking physics."

"Almost flunking," Sarah corrected.

"Okay. Almost, not quite. But I don't understand the connection between her pregnancy and your almost flunking."

Sarah let the book slip off her head. "She was my lab partner."

"Sarah," Alf said, scratching his head. Shirley was suppressing a giggle. "I don't think I'm opaque on these matters, but I am beginning to think that I missed some major point in the old birds-and-bees discussion. I thought that I had received the standard kind of sex education. So far it seems to have worked fairly well. Has there been some recent evolutionary change in sexual reproduction? Do same-sex lab partners now have reproductive capacities? Are you trying to tell me that you are responsible for your lab partner's child?"

Everybody broke up laughing. Shirley got up and slapped Alf's shoulder. "You are so funny!"

"I wasn't trying to be funny," he protested. "I was trying to get an answer out of Sarah as to why she is getting a poor grade in physics."

"Look, guys." Sarah, who had been reclining on the sofa, now slithered off entirely and lay on the floor with her legs hiked up over the armrest. This was her favorite posture for talking to her

175

family at the end of a long, hard day. And it had been just that: In addition to two hours of Christmas pageant rehearsal and the news about Emily, every one of her teachers had been in a cranky mood. Her aunt had just delivered the toddy and sat down in a chair by the sofa, and Sarah was now eye to eye with Hattie's dragons. "You see," Sarah continued, "Emily's really smart and she was my partner for this lab period. Together we were going to do something for the school science fair. Miss Whitman said anyone who did a decent job on a science-fair project could raise their grade, and mine definitely needs to be raised, let me tell you."

"Science fair?" said Alf. "I never knew Stuart Hall had a science fair. Since when?"

"Since five years ago, or whenever it was that the Russians sent up Sputnik. Remember, all of us American youth are supposed to be dummies next to the Russian ones. So the push is on."

"I think it sounds like fun," he said. "What are you going to do?"

"Dad!" Sarah rolled over and propped herself on her elbow. "That's just the problem. It's only three weeks away! I don't know what to do. Emily was supposed to figure that out. The projects could be joint. And now we've been disjointed. Emily's being shipped to a home for unwed mothers in Terre Haute."

"Terre Haute!" Alf exclaimed. "That's where John Dillinger came from."

"We've been through that already," Hattie said.

"Gee," Alf said. "That sounds rather grim, doesn't it? For Emily more than you—if you don't mind my saying so."

"Well, it's not as grim as being entombed," Sarah said.

"Entombed!" Three voices hooted the word in dismay. The dragons tossed their heads and reared as Hattie uncrossed and recrossed her legs.

"That's what they did with vestal virgins—walled them up alive."

"How could we forget?" Shirley said. "I really feel that Miss Ullrich was rather narrow about that report of yours. It was so clever, so well done. I could just see Edward R. Murrow interviewing that poor thing. What was her name?"

"Fabia Livonis. Well, nobody's going to have anything to be narrow about with my science project because it's just not going to be."

"I think it's a shame that a pregnant girl can't finish her education," Alf said.

"Well, I'll tell you, said Sarah, "an unpregnant one is going to have a hard time finishing hers."

"Oh, Alf." Shirley shook her head sadly. "Be realistic. Can you imagine a pregnant teenager walking around Stuart Hall?"

"I agree with Alf." One little dragon head bobbed furiously in frenetic accompaniment to Hattie's voice. "Just think. If Emily didn't have to go, she and Sarah could do a wonderful project on human reproduction."

"Oh, sure, Aunt Hattie! A childbirth exhibit. I could deliver Emily's baby in the gym right next to Hillary Daniels's planaria experiment and Trudy Hollowell's electromagnets. Sure thing—*I Was a Teenage Obstetrician*. Any more ideas?"

Shirley and Alf were laughing. "Listen," Shirley said, shifting in her seat. "There is no way they are going to let Emily Heath stay around. That place is *so* straightlaced. It's not just Crowninshield and the teachers. Some of the parents are even worse. You know that Mrs. Eliot?"

"Anne Eliot's mother?" Sarah asked.

Shirley nodded. "Did you know that she wants to ban *Catcher in the Rye* from the school library?"

"Ban!" The dragons slapped the floor as Aunt Hattie jumped to her feet. "You know, Alf and Shirley, despite Stuart Hall's being a private preparatory school, fancying itself in the tradition of eastern prep schools, there are an awful lot of really tacky people over there. What do they do for fun, burn crosses on people's lawns?"

Sarah lay in bed that night thinking about Emily Heath. She tried to remember what Emily's stomach looked like under her uniform. Had it stuck out at all? She couldn't recall. It was hard for Sarah to imagine anybody doing it, but to imagine Emily going all the way was almost impossible. She was not especially attractive. She wore very ugly glasses: Harlequin-style frames that swooped up and had a few little jewels decorating the outer corners. Her hair wasn't anything to get excited about either: mousy brown, with those awful, tightly crimped bangs—Mamie Eisenhower bangs, they were called. They went out when dowdy Mamie and Ike left the White House and sleek Jackie and Jack moved in. Emily's hairstyle was definitely out-of-date. But beneath the crimped bangs and behind the tilting frames was a generous spirit. She would be a good mother. And although Sarah only partly understood, she began to cry softly.

Her face was streaked with tears, her cheeks slick and burning. Half of her was crying for Emily, her departed lab partner, with whom she had enjoyed a growing new friendship. But half of her was crying for Sarah. It had been all downhill for her this past year, starting with the disastrous Christmas dance; then, in May, Madame's unexpected retirement and return to Paris with her childhood sweetheart, a World War I flying ace; through a broiling summer, during which Marla had only come home for two weeks. Now it was November again: 'Tis the season to be jolly and to be a shepherd—*again*. Since seventh grade she had been a shepherd and nothing else had changed much in the last four years—not since eighth grade anyway. Seventh was almost too long ago to remember, but nothing had changed, at least not in a meaningful way.

Oh yes, there were the usual indicators of certain kinds of growth. Thanks to four years of the text *Word Power Made Easy,* she had probably doubled her vocabulary. And she had mastered quadratic equations and different proofs for the Pythagorean theorem, and had gone from the dynasties of Egypt and Hammurabi's Code to the Louisiana Purchase and considerations of constitutional law. Learning had come in large chunks, and boredom had accumulated in small, steady increments; yet everything was the same. Marla was gone; Hattie flitted in and out of her life. Although she could almost tolerate Hattie now, she still missed Marla.

She suddenly realized how weary she was of wanting and missing. She was beginning her third year of wanting and missing and boredom punctuated by disasters of greater or lesser magnitude that ranged from Ethan Johnson and the Christmas dance to criticisms of impudence in interpreting history (her vestal virgin report) and insolence regarding behavioral codes (the addition of the tenth rule forbidding the fingering of Harvard beets). Disasters. Sarah reflected on the word. In Italian, *disastrato*, ill-starred, "the evil star"; *dis* being the pejorative or negative; *astro* from the Latin *astrum*, meaning "star." Her tears had stopped. She might, she just might, cut school tomorrow. She had never done that in her life. But there was a first time for everything.

# Chapter Twenty-three

The rehearsal had just begun. They were still within the first minute or so, the first few verses of the second chapter of Luke; the dimmers had not even come up yet and the only light onstage fell from the tinfoil star with the bulb plugged into its middle. The star itself was still dimmed to its lowest magnitude. It yielded just enough light to pick a hangnail by, which was exactly what Sarah was doing. She was furious. She had planned to come to school only for first-period French—there was to be a test that she had studied for and didn't want to miss. She had brought along her entire allowance for the month and half of the preceding month's. She still had another two months' allowance at home, since she had bought hardly any clothes lately. When one had to wear uniforms and also had parents who loved to buy clothes, one did save money. She had planned to get sick immediately after the French test, thereby avoiding rehearsal, and to drive "home."

Of course, what she would really do was drive downtown and just mess around. Since she had gotten her driver's license and inherited Marla's old car, she had hardly driven anyplace except school and her friends' homes. It was time she took advantage of this independent means of transport. So much for that! Crowninshield had rearranged the schedule, declaring yesterday's rehearsal a "disaster." That word again, thought Sarah. Maybe that was what happened when one tried to capture the Star of Bethlehem and turn it into a prop for an old lady's ideas about the Gospel of St. Luke, the nativity of Jesus Christ, and a middle-class version of Western civilization as enacted by privileged girls from suburban Indianapolis. It was disaster. To capture a star—it was like trying to capture wild animals and breed them in captivity. Didn't they become infertile, disoriented, and deranged, dying early of broken hearts in "safe" places?

Sarah completed the French test after rehearsal, went to the rest room, made some gagging noises, flushed the toilet, went to Vice Principal St. John's office, and informed her that she was "not at all well," had just thrown up, and would like to go home. Ten minutes later Sarah was cruising south down Capitol Street toward downtown Indianapolis. She felt so free. Even the smell of the air was better. She swung into a White Castle and bought a bagful of burgers and a large Coke. Three White Castle hamburgers were equivalent to one regular hamburger. They cost twenty-two cents apiece, and Sarah bought six. She gobbled three in her car in the parking lot and the rest while driving the short distance downtown. This was a perfect day to cut school. She knew for sure she wouldn't run into any of her mom's friends. They were all on the same boards for the same volunteer groups, and two of the biggies were meeting today: Planned Parenthood in the morning and Meals-on-Wheels in the afternoon. It was driving her mother crazy because she also had a paper due for her finance course, and Sarah thought she had said there was also something else she had to do today. She probably wouldn't see her mom until dinnertime. A languorous day stretched ahead of her. She wanted to look at some new clothes. Maybe cruise wear—the other night her dad had mumbled something about a vacation in the Caribbean.

She parked the car just west of Meridian and walked boldly into Ayre's department store. She gave up the idea of cruise wear as soon as she saw the new Scotch House Shop in the College Girl department. There were wonderful plaid skirts and mohair car coats and shetland sweaters. She bought herself a Black Watch plaid kilt and pale yellow sweater, but she didn't have enough money for the car coat, which she really liked. She could have charged it to her mother's account, but it didn't seem right to put it on your mom's charge on a day you were cutting school. After all, there were ethics to this business of cutting. She had to get some nice knee socks next. She preferred another department store for this. So she cut through notions on the first floor and went out the Washington Street exit.

In Block's she found two pairs of knee socks. She then went to the cosmetic counter and tried out whatever samples were available. She bought herself a new lipstick—Peachy Keen. For old times' sake she thought she would go up to the Tea Room and check out the section reserved for mothers shopping with their children. She and Marla had come there with their own mother countless times as children. You were allowed to pick a present from a grab bag on entering. They also served a special lunch for kids: creamed chicken in an animal-shaped china cup. When she was little she always put in a special request for the Dumbo cup. Dessert was clown sundaes: a scoop of vanilla ice cream with an ice-cream cone hat and candy eyes, the whole deal resting on a vanilla cookie with a whipped-cream collar on a huge puddle of chocolate sauce.

Sarah now passed slowly by the velvet cordon separating the Tea Room from housewares. There were loads of children with their well-turned-out mommies—little girls in jumpers with ribbons in their hair, little boys in blazers or very nice sweaters over tiny oxford shirts. She scanned the tables. Nobody had a Dumbo cup. Marla said you knew you were no longer a child when they wouldn't let you pick a present from the grab bag at Block's and you needed two Dumbos of creamed chicken to feel satisfied at lunch. Next to that area was the regular dining room and then the Men's Grill. What a stupid concept, Sarah thought. Segregated eating! She walked by a sea of dark suits, a lot of gray or balding heads bent in earnest conversation, obviously all plotting development strategies for the business and economic growth of this great heart-of-the-heartland city. Chicago, after all, didn't count. Chicago wasn't really Midwest. It happened to be located there, slightly west of Indianapolis, but in its heart it was East. As cities go—eastern cities, that is—it was bustling and bossy and rude and feverish. Whereas Indianapolis had its own plodding rhythm that was distinctly Midwest. None of the languorousness of a southern city. No, Indianapolis worked at a flat, predictable, no-nonsense pace. There would be growth, but it would not be that horrid, willynilly, sprawling kind of scablike growth that covered eastern states with housing projects and shopping malls. It would not, on the other hand, be especially aesthetic either. As for charm, well, some people might call Indianapolis charmless, but the natives would say, "No, we just don't lay it on like some folks pour syrup on pancakes. The charm is there—you just have to find it." Sarah studied the Men's Grill. Suddenly one man's face, a face she knew, lifted and beamed at her. She should have remembered. Her dad's good friend Paul Mode ran the menswear department. He had gotten up and, waving madly, was making his way between the diners.

"Hi, sweetie! What brings you down here?" He kissed her.

"Paul! Oh, Paul! Please don't tell my parents."

"You're cutting school. I would never have guessed," Paul said.

"You know, I've never ever done this. This is my first time ever, and . . ."

"Well, what the heck's wrong with you, kiddo? Listen, when

I was in high school—you know, back in the Paleozoic—I made a habit of cutting at least once a month. Come on, Sarah, you're a junior. You've got a lot of catching up to do." Then he gave her shoulders a squeeze. "Don't worry, kid. I won't tell anybody. Mum's the word. By the way, did you see the Christmas windows on Illinois Street?"

"No, I came in through the other entrance."

"Do me a favor. Go see. We spent a fortune. It was such aggravation. But we've got it working now. It's a Tyrolean village with Pinocchio, Snow White, the seven dwarfs, the elves and the shoemaker—the whole shebang. It's so much better than Ayre's. You know they always do that North Pole–Santa Claus–Rudolph stuff. This is really artistic, let me tell you! Promise me you'll go out the Illinois Street exit."

"I promise."

That, Sarah supposed, was the charm of Indianapolis: You cut school, you run into your dad's best friend downtown, he not only promises not to tell on you but makes *you* promise to look at the Christmas windows.

After looking at the display, Sarah cut through an alley behind Block's to get her car. There was a row of big trash bins against one wall, and propped on top was what Sarah first thought was a piece of glass. Through it she could see a discarded magazine with John Kennedy's picture on the cover. But then with great shock she realized that her own image was being reflected back. She stopped and stared. Her reflection was mingled so completely with Kennedy's that it was hard to tell which was which. She walked up to the bin and picked up the fragment. It was nothing more than a piece of half-silvered glass, maybe from an old window display. Behind it lay a copy of *Life* magazine with Kennedy on the cover. She put down her shopping bag and propped up the magazine.

184

Then she held the mirror up between herself and the magazine. The piece of glass, about twelve inches square, functioned as both a window and a mirror. Standing in front of it Sarah could see herself reflected in the "mirror," but if she looked through the "window" she could see the image of Kennedy. The images mingled and overlapped. The effect was stunning and hypnotic. Sarah realized suddenly, with pleasant alarm, that this would be her science project.

She arrived home shortly before Shirley. She had not expected her mother home so soon.

"What are you doing here?" Sarah asked. "I thought you had Meals-on-Wheels."

"That's over with. I'm just here to change my shoes, which are killing me, before I go to the censorship meeting at Stuart Hall."

"What, you're going to school?"

"Yes. Didn't I tell you that I'm spearheading the anticensorship drive over *Catcher in the Rye*? We can't have idiots like that Eliot woman running around banning books."

Oh gosh, St. John would ask her mother how Sarah was feeling and there she'd be—caught. Why did she have to have a spearhead for a mother! Sarah thought rapidly. "Did I tell you that I threw up today?"

Shirley stopped massaging her feet. "What? You're sick?"

"Not exactly—but I did come home early from school."

Shirley looked perplexed. "Well, how come you're still in your uniform?"

There was not going to be any really good way out of this. Sarah sighed. "Well, uh . . . The problem is, I didn't exactly throw up. I kind of faked throwing up."

"You faked throwing up?" Shirley repeated.

"Yeah, because I am in a sense really sick—sick of school, that is. And— Oh gosh, Mom, I just couldn't stand one more Christmas pageant rehearsal, so I cut."

"You cut! You cut school!" Shirley stared in disbelief.

"Mom, it's really not that bad." To Sarah she seemed excessively shocked.

"Well, I know it's not that bad, Sarah, but I'm surprised. I don't think anybody in our family has ever cut school before."

"Paul Mode told me he cut at least once a month when he was in high school."

"Paul Mode? Where'd you see him?"

"Block's."

"Block's? What did you do, have lunch in the Men's Grill?"

"No, I just ran into him there."

"Just your luck to cut and run into a family friend." Shirley laughed.

"Yeah, I know, but he promised not to tell anybody."

"He promised that?" Shirley's eyes widened.

"Yeah. He's so nice."

"Maybe, but what am I supposed to say at school?"

"Just tell them I'm feeling better and I'll be back tomorrow. That's the truth. You won't have to lie. And don't worry, Mom. I didn't miss anything in school. I stayed for my French test and, because I cut, I figured out my science-fair project, which I almost literally stumbled across when I came out of Block's."

"What's that?"

"It's this really neat thing. It's a piece of glass. You can see through it and yet it reflects, too."

"Can you turn it into an exhibit in time for the fair?" Shirley asked.

"Sure. I've got nearly three weeks to set it up. It's all about reflections, and transmitting light and images, and——"

"Well," Shirley interrupted, "I guess it was worth it, then. I'll be back in time for dinner. I thought I'd just pick up some Chinese food—that is, if your delicate stomach can take it. Hattie may or may not be here for dinner. That reminds me—she'll have her apartment renovation finished by the first week in December and she's got Lieba and Shlomo set up for all sorts of East Coast dates starting at Christmas. They'll be able to move into their new place as soon as they come back from Israel. So we'll be seeing much less of Hattie. I'll miss her terribly. I know you won't."

"Well, it's been a long two years, but I've gotten used to her. She doesn't bug me as much anymore."

"See, you're maturing!" Sarah made a face at this comment. "Okay, dear, I'll be back soon. I don't relish this censorship thing."

"Then why are you doing it?"

"Sarah! You amaze me. Don't you think there is something fundamentally wrong, basically ignorant, about trying to ban a book? I mean, we're talking about the First Amendment here!"

"Yeah, I know."

"Somebody has to fight these things."

Sarah wasn't sure why it had to be her mother. She preferred mothers who were slightly anonymous.

"Listen," Sarah said, "be sure to get at least ten spring rolls when you stop at Wu's—Aunt Hattie is such a pig about spring rolls. She always eats more than her share."

"Okay. Wish me luck, darling. That Mrs. Eliot is a real dragon."

"Okay. So long, St. George, and don't forget the spring rolls."

187

# Chapter Twenty-four

Dear Marla,

Mom just went out to slay the dragon of censorship, which has appeared at Stuart Hall in the form of Anne Eliot's mother. *Catcher in the Rye* is the book in question. The whole Eliot family is a bunch of congenital creeps, so I don't know why Mom wants to do battle with them. Well, yes I do. It's the First Amendment. All very admirable. She's so busy these days between her business-school stuff, her Planned Parenthood board (They missed one with Emily Heath—she got pregnant, and she was supposed to be my physics lab partner!), and her Meals-on-Wheels. A little baby died on Daddy the other night. When something like that happens, you can always tell as soon as he walks in the door: His left eyelid has a way of drooping, and his footsteps sound—I don't know—slow and flat.

Aunt Hattie apparently moves back to New York permanently the first week in December. Can you believe that I have successfully restrained her for over two years from painting the bathroom crème de ca-ca!

I think I've come up with a good idea for the science fair. I'm using a half-silvered glass. It reflects and transmits and is like a combination window and mirror. It's real weird to see how your reflection combines with someone else's on the other side. I thought I would build some sort of stand and hang it up, and people could come up and try it out. Remember how in *Through the Looking Glass*

Alice talks about how all the reflections are behind the glass and not on its surface? She says, " 'Let's pretend that the glass has got all soft like gauze, so that we can get through. . . .' " And then it turns sort of misty and they go through. That's exactly what this mirror is like. I have a feeling that there is some sort of moral in all this somewhere—like we're all alike no matter how different. I'd better watch it. That'll never fly at Stuart Hall. Got to run now.

Love, Sarah

What did not fly at the science fair was the questionnaire Sarah had written to accompany the project. The questionnaire attempted to fathom people's response to having their image mingled with others'. When people approached the exhibit Sarah would ask if they would like to sit opposite a friend or herself, one on the silvered side, the other on the clear side of the mirror. Next Sarah would suspend a portrait rigged from a coat hanger on the clear side of the glass. The pictures had been taken from old *Time* or *Life* magazines and included photographs of famous public figures ranging from John Kennedy to Mickey Mouse. People could then see their face in combination with one of these figures. Afterward Sarah would hand them a brief questionnaire to fill out.

### THE BENJAMIN COMFORT SCALE
### FOR THE COMMINGLING OF IMAGES

Thank you for participating in my project: "Variations on Alice's Looking Glass." In an attempt to ascertain levels of comfort as participants observe their own faces combined with those of well-known personages, I would very much appreciate your completion of this brief questionnaire. All results will be kept strictly confidential. You need not put your name on this questionnaire, but it is pertinent for the data that you enter your age, sex, and race in the blanks below. Then please proceed to circle the number that best indicates your mental comfort at the time your reflection combined with that of the persons listed below. One indicates the lowest level of comfort; five indicates the highest.

age: _____

sex: _____

race: _____

| | | | | | |
|---|---|---|---|---|---|
| John Kennedy | 1 | 2 | 3 | 4 | 5 |
| Sophia Loren | 1 | 2 | 3 | 4 | 5 |
| Rev. Billy Graham | 1 | 2 | 3 | 4 | 5 |
| Grace Kelly | 1 | 2 | 3 | 4 | 5 |
| Mickey Mouse | 1 | 2 | 3 | 4 | 5 |
| Rev. Martin Luther King | 1 | 2 | 3 | 4 | 5 |
| Bob Hope | 1 | 2 | 3 | 4 | 5 |
| Pope John XXIII | 1 | 2 | 3 | 4 | 5 |

Sarah had set up her exhibit between Hillary Daniels's experiment and Jessie Cavanaugh's solar reflector, on which she had broiled a hamburger the previous summer. Jesse had hung photographs above the exhibit showing the hamburger turning from raw to well-done. Hillary had more or less broiled planaria. Her father was a dentist, and he had X-rayed countless petri dishes filled with planaria for her to study on the effect of radiation on reproduction.

Miss Crowninshield had come by about thirty minutes after the fair started. She sat down on the mirror side of the glass and Miss Patchet, the school secretary, was enlisted to sit down on the window side. All went well. When Miss Patchet got up, Sarah brought down the picture of Grace Kelly. That was fine. John Kennedy brought out a tiny frown; Sophia Loren, and Miss Crowninshield peered harder—"very exotic eyes," she whispered; then Mickey Mouse—she giggled: "Oh, how cute!" Then Martin Luther King. There was a definite wince and a scowl. Minus-one on the comfort scale, Sarah thought. No wonder last year's senior gift had been vetoed: Instead of the two hundred dollars being used as starter money for a scholarship fund for black students, it had gone to purchase a clock for the study hall.

"Hrrumph," Miss Crowninshield growled. "What are you calling this effort, Sarah?" Sarah was busily trying to lower the picture of Bob Hope, but the hanger had snagged on something. "Effort!" Obviously Miss Crowninshield was not regarding this as *science*. No, *science* was Jessie Cavanaugh's ground-beef photos. *Science* was Hillary's X-rayed planaria. It was Elaine's molds, which could still reproduce after spending days in vials of liquid nitrogen at $-248°$ Fahrenheit. Having your features mingled with those of Sophia Loren, Mickey Mouse, and, God forbid, Martin Luther King was not *science,* but miscegenation—mixing of bloods! Sarah could talk until she was blue in the face about reflection, transmission waves, grains and particles of light, refraction, images, mirages, shadows and illusions, as she had in her long, written explanation and background material on the project, but forget it! Forget that there was a physics for all this. Crowninshield's view of the universe did not include either the paradox or the prejudice Sarah had demonstrated by her window-mirror project. As Sarah had observed since she had first been drafted for the pageant in the seventh grade, in Crowninshield's world angels always had blonde hair and blue eyes and the Virgin Mary a soprano voice; shepherds had tangles of unruly dark hair or at least violent auburn like Phoebe's and no singing voices. In such a universe there was little room for unexpected molecular movement, for oddities in the reflection or transmission of light, or, heaven forbid, of attitude.

Sarah hesitated. "I'm calling it 'Variations on Alice's Looking Glass.' It's sort of a perceptual study as related to reflection and transmission of light. Here's my statement of purpose." Sarah handed Miss Crowninshield a mimeographed sheet and a questionnaire. "You could fill out the questionnaire if you like."

Miss Crowninshield looked briefly at the two sheets and then stomped across the aisle to Betsy Fuller's eighteen million generations of fruit flies.

Ten minutes later Sarah noticed Miss Crowninshield huddled in a corner of the gym with Miss Whitman. She knew in her gut that they were reading over the sheets Sarah had given to Crowninshield. Then she saw Miss Whitman walking toward her.

"Sarah." The old face was plump and grayish, and little wire-rim glasses perched on her nearly bridgeless nose. "Sarah." She began again and scratched her head, which had very little hair on it. "I'm afraid that after some discussion with Miss Crowninshield we are going to have to ask that you not hand out those questionnaires."

"What!" Sarah was stunned. "But I don't understand, Miss Whitman. It puts a nice finish on the study. You're always talking about that—a 'nice finish' and 'good recording devices.' It sort of draws into perspective the focus on the project."

"Yes . . . yes. But as Miss Crowninshield pointed out, you are actually mixing two disciplines here—physics and psychology." Sarah could tell that all this was quite difficult for Miss Whitman, who was shy and too kind and therefore mincemeat in Crowninshield's hands. "You are making it unnecessarily complicated, Sarah."

"No I'm not. This questionnaire is a genuine part of the project. You know that. You're a scientist."

Miss Whitman stopped wringing her plump hands and looked down at them as she spoke.

"Sarah, this is the way it has to be. Now, we are not asking you to take down the exhibit. Just hand over the questionnaires to me."

Yesterday J. D. Salinger and *Catcher in the Rye;* today S. E. Benjamin and "Variations on Alice's Looking Glass," she thought.

"I just don't understand," she pleaded.

"I'm not asking you to understand. Just give me the questionnaires!" Miss Whitman hissed. Then her voice became softer. "Sarah, don't worry, your grade will be raised."

Sarah looked Miss Whitman straight in the face, straight beyond her own image as it was reflected in the two lenses of Miss Whitman's glasses, straight to the faded and weary brown eyes. "Are you trying to buy me off, Miss Whitman?"

Sarah turned and left. She walked past Hillary and the irradiated planaria, past Elaine and the thawed, reproducing bread molds, past the model of the atom built with Ping-Pong balls, past two rats in a maze.

That night Hattie came in and sat on the edge of Sarah's bed. She sighed deeply. "Stuart Hall is never going to be called the Athens of the Midwest."

"You heard?" Sarah said.

"I sure did. I think it's rotten." Hattie sighed again and for the first time ever she slid her eye patch up and rubbed the red and crinkled depression. "Oh gee, I'm sorry." She quickly apologized and repositioned the patch.

"Don't worry," Sarah said. "It didn't bother me."

"Was it as bad as you thought?" Hattie whispered in a small voice.

"No, no. Don't worry, Aunt Hattie."

How strange, Sarah thought, her telling The Hat not to worry.

"Anyway," Hattie continued. "Just remember, Sarah, that in 1633 the pope made Galileo recant his position on the earth moving around the sun; then only one hundred years later they reversed their opinion and said he was right, that indeed the earth did move around the sun."

"Oh, that's very heartening, Aunt Hattie." Now it was Sarah who sighed.

"Did they show you the torture equipment, dear?" Sarah giggled. Hattie continued. "You know that's what they did with Galileo: took him down to the Vatican dungeons—probably not the Swiss Guard, just some papal thugs. They took him down there to show him the rack, you know, the press and the screw, assorted other goodies. He said, 'Hey, guys, I know how this stuff works—you're right. The sun goes around the earth.' "

Sarah laughed. "No, they didn't show me the torture equipment. Basically they bought me off with a raised grade, but I might not accept it."

Hattie's eye danced. "Really, Sarah!"

"Well, there wasn't much I could do about the questionnaires. They would simply have confiscated them. It's the principle of the thing that bugs me."

"Good for you, Sarah! You really are a principled person—truly in the tradition of Jack Kennedy and the New Frontier!"

"Oh, Aunt Hattie, it's so neat of you to say that!" She squeezed her aunt's hand, and Hattie leaned over to kiss her good-night. Her eye patch brushed Sarah's cheek. "You, Sarah Eloise Benjamin, are going to go forth with great vigor—once you get out of that school!"

# Chapter Twenty-five

" ' And it came to pass, as the angels were gone away from them into heaven, the shepherds said one to another . . .' "

"Do you realize," Sarah whispered, "that we have spent one hundred and sixteen hours of our lives being a heap of sleeping shepherds in the Christmas pageant?"

"You're kidding," Phoebe muttered.

"You've spent more, Phoebe, because you're a year older." Sarah had just finished calculating her rehearsal time from 1959, when she had first become a shepherd in the seventh grade, to 1963. At first the number did not seem particularly significant, but then she realized that this represented almost five days of life. If she had been born a mayfly, which only lives one day, she would have spent her entire lifetime rehearsing for a Christmas pageant, or doing whatever is equally boring for a mayfly. The remaining four days she would have been dead. It was really just exchanging one kind of death for another.

According to an article in one of her father's medical journals, during the average lifespan all mammals have nearly the same number of breaths and heartbeats. It is just the pace that varies. Some burn fast—mouse and shrew; some burn slow—whale and elephant; Homo sapiens get a little more time than their size would suggest. But the ratio of breath to pulse is roughly 1:4, or one breath for every four heartbeats. The question now, as Sarah saw it, was: How did one spend those beats and breaths? She had more time than the mayfly or small mammals, but in terms of the number of heartbeats their lifespans were not that different. The light from the tinfoil star seemed now to fall directly upon the heap of shepherds. She could feel her own heart beating. She could watch the rhythmic rising and falling of the cheesecloth robes. Sarah felt her heart beat faster, her breath become shallow and quick. The numbers were dwindling even as she "slept."

Hillary was counting down. "Two."

"Get ready!"

" 'Let us now go even unto Bethlehem—' "

And with great vigor! Sarah thought as the shepherds began to stir.

" '—and see this thing' "—Miss Crowninshield pumped up the wonder quotient in her voice—" 'which is come to pass, which the Lord hath made known unto us.' "

"One." And then the chorus began.

"Shepherds, shake off your drowsy sleep.
Rise, and leave your silly sheep;
Angels from heav'n around are singing,
Tidings of great joy are bringing."

Hillary always went first, stopping just beyond the manger and turning toward it. Sarah was second, Phoebe Buxton third, and then Elaine. Except this time Phoebe stopped a foot or so short of her normal position, which was marked by a chalked *X* on the floor, as she watched Sarah walk straight off the stage. The maroon-robed figure simply vanished into the wings.

"What's wrong?" Drusilla Benson, the curtain puller, asked as Sarah walked by her.

"Just a little shortness of breath," Sarah said, and kept on walking. She went to her locker and put on her pea jacket over her robes. She took her pocketbook and left her books and crook and walked straight out the exit to the parking lot. The cold November wind snapped at her face. She remembered that she had two months' allowance in her pocketbook because she had planned to go downtown after school to buy that mohair car coat in Ayre's College Girl department. That's it! thought Sarah, the perfect excuse and the money. She could go far, farther actually than Ayre's and the mohair car coat. Her parents knew she was going shopping and wouldn't expect her home until late. She would call Elaine and get her to cover for her. Elaine owed her one. She had covered for Elaine just last week when Elaine was supposed to be studying at Sarah's house and had instead gone out with Stephen. If she drove straight through she could make it to New York in under two days, and that was exactly what she intended to do. She was tired of missing Marla. And that was all that Sarah knew about what she was doing or why she was doing it.

Two blocks east on Washington Street she stopped at a phone booth.

"Oh, hi, Miss Patchet." Fortunately the call was answered by Miss Patchet, who trusted everybody. "Listen, I got sick during rehearsal and I came home. I threw up all over myself so I didn't want to come into the office for formal permission to leave. . . . Oh, oh good, thanks for understanding. Listen, I forgot some important homework and I have to explain to Elaine Bauer exactly which notebook to look for in my locker. She knows the combination. Could you please get Elaine? . . . Thanks, Miss Patchet."

While she waited, Sarah lined up more dimes for the phone.

"Listen, Elaine . . ." When the operator interrupted, Sarah slid in twenty cents.

"Where are you, Sarah?"

"Look, don't worry. Don't ask too many questions. Just remember I covered for you and Stephen last week. I need your help now."

"Sure. Do you have a secret boyfriend?" Elaine asked with anticipation.

"No, no. Listen to this carefully. I'm going to call my house and leave a message with the cleaning lady that we're going shopping together and I'm going to spend the night at your house, and that I won't be home until late tomorrow afternoon because we have to distribute the Thanksgiving canned goods to the families in need. Just back me up on this, okay?"

"Okay, Sarah, but what are you doing?"

"Don't worry about what I'm doing. It's okay."

"All right," Elaine said. "Good luck, whatever it is."

One more phone call and Sarah had effectively completed the fabrication—the lie. Face it, she thought, you're lying, but only to save yourself, save your heartbeats and not squander them, at least. When you get to Marla's you can call home and tell them that you're safe, sound, and self-abducted. That's it! she thought as she headed due east on Route 40. It was twelve noon, November 21, 1963, and she was on the road. You're not a runaway. You're a self-abductee saving yourself from terminal boredom, not to mention moral corruption in the form of grade bribery in exchange for violations of the First Amendment in a polluted, so-called intellectual environment.

The highway was the same one she and Lieba and Elaine had traveled almost two years before. But now there was no snow. The road was clear and straight. She was past Greenfield in no time. Within an hour and a half she had crossed the Indiana–Ohio border. She was careful to keep within the speed limit. All she needed was to get stopped for speeding. Her gas tank had been full when she left. There were road maps in the glove compartment, in fact an old AAA Triptik from when her mom and Marla had first driven East to look at colleges. But the highways were pretty well marked and she did not have to rely very heavily on the maps. Her goal was to get a "foot in the door" of Pennsylvania before really taking a rest. She stopped just over the state line for gas. At thirty-five cents a gallon, five bucks filled the tank. She bought several Cokes and candy bars. It had been just before this stop that she realized she was still wearing her shepherd's costume. She had ripped off the burnoose while driving, and when she stopped for the gas she took off the robes. She was tempted to put them in a trash can but she had seen enough movies to know better than to leave such obvious tracks.

She gave very little thought to what Marla would say. Marla would be surprised, of course, but she knew that delight would immediately follow. She pictured herself running into Marla's arms and Marla's understanding everything—the 116 hours of pageant rehearsal, the allotted heartbeats, the First Amendment violations, the boredom—ah, *Marla* would understand the boredom.

Sarah negotiated the tricky interchange around Columbus with great skill. Route 70, which she had been traveling since entering Ohio about an hour ago, crossed with about a zillion other roads as one got within ten miles of Columbus. But she did manage to avoid downtown Columbus. This was a major driving coup. At eight-thirty, just when she would normally be in the middle of her homework, she saw her first sign for Pittsburgh: ninety miles. She was so thrilled with her accomplishment that she felt only a twinge of homesickness when she thought of her parents and Aunt Hattie sitting down to watch "Perry Mason." And although they might not understand right now, they would, they would! She was convinced of this. Hadn't Hattie said that she had principles—like the New Frontierspeople? that she would go forth with great vigor? She was merely going forth a little earlier than scheduled. She eased up on the accelerator and watched the speedometer slide under eighty again. She would be a hero. Well, not quite a hero. Don't overdo it, Sarah, she counseled herself. She would be what she was—a self-abducted, principled person, an incipient New Frontiersperson.

Amazingly enough, she felt no fatigue, not even hunger. Her metabolism was working at a rate more fitting for small mammals. But who cared? She was on the move, not merely driving but captaining this car, navigating her way eastward—to Marla!

She arrived in Pittsburgh near eleven that night, having unfortunately missed a sign that would have routed her around the city. It was close to midnight when she finally got squared away. At one she decided to pull off the turnpike at a service area near Willow Hill, Pennsylvania, and take a nap. She wasn't really tired, but felt she should rest a bit in order to keep her driving reflexes sharp. She slept for three hours. The Howard Johnson's at the service area was open all night. She went in and ordered some scrambled eggs and English muffins. She bought gas for the car, and by four-thirty she was on the road again.

There was a lot of truck traffic, big semis. At five in the morning a light drizzle began, making the roads slick. She slackened her pace. It was lucky she had rested: The driving was much more demanding now. "Real George Washington weather," she muttered as she passed a sign for Valley Forge. A thick fog rolled up the highway and slowed traffic to a snail's pace for nearly half an hour. Flashing warning lights indicated hazardous driving conditions. She crossed the Delaware at nine-thirty that morning, just when the bell for second period would be ringing at Stuart Hall. This last stretch seemed to take forever. She got horribly mixed up trying to get onto the New Jersey Turnpike. At one point she actually almost recrossed the Delaware. "Oh gosh! What would George say!" she muttered. She didn't know what road she was on. For hours it seemed as if she drove in circles and repeatedly passed the sign for Walt Whitman's home. Camden was like a giant magnet for her car. Put her on any road and she was drawn back to Camden. She pulled into a gas station and studied the map. Finally, near one in the afternoon she found the New Jersey Turnpike.

Well, she thought, one major navigational error isn't so bad. She decided to see if she could get a New York radio station. She turned the dial. Hymn music on the first station; more hymn music. What was it, Sunday? Then she heard a newscaster's staticky voice.

"The word here, Henry, is that the President has been——" She switched the station. Another voice: "The mood at Parkland Hospital is somber. There has been no word——" More hymns as she switched. She turned the dial further. "President Kennedy has been shot. . . . A spokesman at the . . ." Sarah's foot jerked away from the accelerator. She shivered as if she had caught the first tremors of an earthquake. "What?" Sarah whispered. "Oh no! Oh no!" Her foot turned to jelly, her hands shook on the wheel. She somehow steered the car to the side of the road. She turned the radio up. There was a man's voice straining to remain calm. "President John F. Kennedy died at approximately one P.M. Central Standard Time today, here in Dallas. He died of a gunshot wound in the brain."

"My God! My God!" Sarah collapsed against the steering wheel. "My God! My God!" No tears came, but her body sobbed, heaving against the steering wheel. When she hit the horn, she barely heard its blare. She merely clutched the wheel tighter as if to hang on through the convulsions of history itself. "No-no-no!" she muttered, and then screamed, "No!" Her vision blurred.

"Henry, everything is still pretty much in a state of confusion here at the hospital. We do know that several doctors worked on the President for several minutes, the better part of a half hour—including a Dr. Malcolm Perry, a surgeon, and Dr. William Kemp Clark, Parkland's chief neurologist. At approximately twelve-fifty-seven two Roman Catholic priests were summoned. . . ." There was a pause, then some static. "Well, Terry—" The newscaster's voice seemed numbed. "Yes. . . ." "We know that you—" His voice broke.

Sarah curled up tight on the front seat. She had never in her life felt more frightened, more alone. She had to get to a phone and call her parents. She could not be alone now. She felt as if the earth had been blown apart and she were a tiny fragment expelled to a remote quarter of a strange galaxy.

She sat up and wiped her eyes. She would drive to the next service station and find a phone.

Within a mile she reached a station. She pulled over and saw the attendants huddled inside. Maybe it was all a mistake. She walked into the office. Three men in grease-stained overalls stood around a desk. The radio played the same tragic story. The older man let the tears run unchecked down his cheeks. A younger one inhaled furiously on a cigarette. The third stood with one shoulder hunched against the wall, his hands gripping his face in a bloodless gesture of torment.

"It's true?" Sarah whispered hoarsely. The three nodded.

"Where's your phone? I've got to call my . . . mommy." The last word came out ever so softly.

The young man extended his cigarette toward a pay phone on the wall. The crying old man said, "Use this one," and shoved the desk phone toward her.

Sarah dialed 0. There was static and all sorts of strange noises. She pressed the button and tried again. A tinny, distant voice came on, tersely explaining that the circuits were all in use. Sarah hung up. She said woodenly, "Can't get an operator."

"All the lines will be jammed, miss. Better try later."

"Yes," she said. "Thank you anyway." She returned to her car.

Three more times she tried along the Jersey Turnpike, but there was no getting through. She kept the radio on. A stream of details began to come through. The shots had been fired from the sixth-floor window of the Texas School Book Depository. A suspect had slipped through a police officer's hands. An officer had been wounded. No, was dead—an Officer Tipton, or Tippit, had died. Air Force One was about to take off from Dallas's Love Field with the unsworn new president, his wife, Jacqueline Kennedy, and the casket bearing the slain president.

Sarah thought that she would never get used to the language: "slain president," "widow," "assassination." As she headed into the darkness of the Lincoln Tunnel she knew there would never be a day for the rest of her life that she would not think of this terrible thing: that John Kennedy had been cut down—"killed dead," she whispered. All his brightness dimmed forever. Oh how many of her own heartbeats, her own breaths she would have given for him.

She began to cry again, softly. "Nothing's fair," she whispered. "No fair! No fair!" She felt so stupid, like a child rankled over some petty injustice. But she just kept muttering "no fair" to herself. Like some syncopated litany, it hammered in her brain. As soon as she was out of the tunnel she spotted a policeman. He was directing traffic in a kind of vague, mechanical manner. She stopped next to him and rolled down her window.

"What can I do for you, miss?" He looked in. His eyes were red-rimmed.

She told him Marla's address and asked how to get there.

"Okay, miss, this won't be so hard. Go straight up the West

Side Highway here until you get to the Seventy-second Street exit. Turn right." Carefully he spelled out the directions. "You got that?" he asked, looking at her rather closely. "You'll do okay?"

"Yeah," Sarah said.

He reached in and put his hand on her shoulder. "Terrible day! terrible day!"

It seemed to Sarah that there was an oddness about the city. Small groups of people stood about on street corners or walked slowly, without apparent purpose, like stunned survivors from a battlefield. The streets were so quiet that through her half-open window Sarah could hear the voices from other people's radios. At a stoplight a black boy walked listlessly with a bag of old newspapers—that morning's newspapers, which might as well be a hundred years old now. He looked at Sarah as she rolled down her window at the red light. He walked up to her open window. A huge tear made a dark, glossy path down his cheek. "What're we gonna do, miss? What're we gonna do?"

He couldn't have been more than ten. His eyes were two pools of darkest sorrow. His hand rested lightly on the doorframe. Sarah looked in the eyes and saw her own reflection. "I don't know." She put her left hand on top of his. And until the light changed to green she rested it there.

# Chapter Twenty-six

"Sarah!" Marla cried, flinging her arms around her sister.

They sobbed in each other's arms. Sarah was vaguely aware of another presence, but she and Marla were so inextricably swirled together that she did not even hear the other person speaking. Together the sisters somehow shuffled inside and collapsed in a heap on the couch. Only when they drew apart did Sarah see the young man standing by the door and looking thoroughly confused.

"Sarah, what in the world are you doing here?" Marla quickly turned to the young man. "Pinchas, this is my sister." In that brief instant, just when Marla turned to speak to the young man, Sarah realized that she was no longer a self-abductee but just a plain runaway. In a few short hours the whole world had been turned upside down, topsy-turvy, as if the magnetic poles had slipped and there was nothing to go toward anymore—no going forth with vigor. There was only away now—away from blood, away from chaos, as an evil star climbed the heavens. *Disastrato!*

"It's a long story." Sarah gulped.

"Do Mom and Dad know where you are?"

Sarah shook her head. "They think I'm at Elaine's or I guess delivering food for the needy by now."

"Sarah! They must be frantic. We've got to call them!"

"The circuits are all busy," Sarah said softly.

"Marla, what is the number?" the young man said, in a lightly accented voice.

"Who's he?" Sarah asked.

"That's Pinchas, my friend Pinchas Rozans."

"Pinchas!" muttered Sarah. What kind of a name is Pinchas? she thought, but asked only, "What's he doing here?"

Marla and Pinchas looked quickly at each other. "The phone number is 317-555-1314, Pinky."

Pinky! She cannot actually call him Pinky! That's disgusting.

Pinchas dialed, waited, then put down the receiver. "She's right. The circuits are still busy. The lines are jammed."

"Is there a bathroom in this place? I don't think I've gone since crossing the Delaware."

"Sarah, you drove!" Marla was dumbfounded.

"Yep. Where's the bathroom?"

In a trance Marla pointed.

She had just finished washing her hands when she noticed the tube with the word *spermicidal*. It was sticking out of a cunning flower-print bag. It was as if Sarah were watching her own brain work in slow motion as she laboriously assembled bits and pieces of information into concepts: They kill sperm here. Who has sperm? Pinchas has sperm. Why do they need to kill sperm? So babies won't grow. Where? In Marla! She put her hand in the bag and drew out a small plastic case. Her hands were trembling. She knew what she would find, but she just had to see it. She opened the case. There sat the little dome of rubber—a diaphragm. *Yuck!* There was a tap on the door. It opened. Marla stood there, pale. Sarah didn't try to hide what she was looking at.

"You know what that is, Sarah?" she asked softly.

Sarah sighed. "What do you think—I was born yesterday?" A rather ironic comment to make, she thought, while holding a birth-control device. "Besides, not for nothing has Mom been on the Planned Parenthood board. She has books and pamphlets about this all over the house."

She was desperately trying to sound casual and knowledgeable.

"So you understand?" Marla asked, sounding relieved.

"Yes, of course," Sarah said tensely. "Now please shut the door. I'm not finished."

"Sure," Marla said.

Sarah grasped the rim of the sink. Yes, she understood. She understood that her sister and Pinchas were . . . She came out of the bathroom. Marla was in the tiny kitchen.

"Do Mom and Dad know?" Sarah asked.

"What?"

What? What? How could she say what? "That you're doing it with him." She refused to say that creepy name of his.

"You mean living with Pinchas?"

Living with him? Maybe there was some sort of hope. Maybe they were just living together and not really doing it.

"Is he living here, too?"

"Yes, he is. And no, Sarah, Mom and Dad do not know about it. All they know is that I've been seeing an Israeli cellist."

"Oh yeah." Now she remembered something about this. But it had all been rather vague. Sarah was dying to ask point-blank, just to have it verbally confirmed, whether they were doing it while they were living together. Was there any chance that they weren't? "Uh, tell me, Marla, is it weird?"

"Is what weird?"

"Not being a virgin?"

Marla giggled. "No."

Something in Sarah crumbled.


Pinchas and Marla had gone out to get groceries for dinner. Sarah said she was tired and preferred to rest. But she could not rest in the apartment. She could not even bear to look at the sleeping alcove with the double bed. She knew that she could not stay another minute.

Three minutes later she stepped out onto West End Avenue. Where could she go? Lieba was still in Israel with Shlomo and the baby. She stood on the sidewalk staring, but not really focusing on anything, until a young woman walked by with a bag slung over her shoulder. A magazine sticking partway out of the bag showed a photo of a ballerina's feet en pointe. The girl was a dancer. Sarah would have known it even if she had not seen the magazine. She could tell by her carriage—the way she walked; her clothes—the thick leg warmers, the tennis shoes. Vronsky! If I follow this girl— But that was nonsense. She did not have to follow anyone. Sarah knew where Vronsky lived: 641 Central Park West, to be exact. She had mailed a package to him from Aunt Hattie only three days ago. She could have delivered it herself!

Within fifteen minutes she was patiently explaining to a very fancily uniformed doorman that she was not another balletomane come to leave a token of adoration. At last in exasperation Sarah blurted out, "Does the name Hattie Silverman mean anything to you?"

"Why, of course," the doorman said, with sudden respect. "You are a friend of Madame Silverman's?"

"I am Madame Silverman's niece from Indianapolis." Sarah felt dignity enfold her like a full-length mocha mink cape.

"This way, miss!"

*"Saar*-ah!" Serge cried as she stepped directly from the paneled elevator to his foyer and stood blinking at its elaborate, tooled-leather walls. "My God, child!" His face was puffy, his eyes red. He opened his arms and engulfed her. "Vat has happened? Could anything more be wrong on this dreadful day? Are you all right?" He

half carried her into his living room, which was about the size of a basketball court. The walls were covered in striped velvet, and on the floor were oriental rugs. Two deep sofas longer than Marla's entire apartment were set at right angles to one another.

"Vat is going on?" Vronsky asked as he sank onto one of the sofas.

"It's a long story."

And so she told him. It all came tumbling out: the campaign button in the pageant three years before, then Marla's leaving, Hattie's coming, Ethan Johnson, Disneyland, Emily Heath, the censored physics project. Sarah began to sniffle. The sniffle built to a sob. She dug into her uniform pocket and brought out a small, tattered piece of Kleenex that was adequate for a doll's nose. She saw Serge watching her as he raised his hand in a gesture of summons. An elderly Chinese man seemed to materialize from behind a jungle of potted ferns. Serge whispered something to the man, who then scurried away. Within a minute he had returned with a stack of ivory-colored handkerchiefs.

"Here, Saar-ah dear." Vronsky shook out a handkerchief and held it toward her.

"Don't you have any Kleenex?"

"Of course not! Vat do you think I am?"

"But I'll mess it all up."

"That's vat it is for. Blow." Even the Chinese man seemed to nod, encouraging her to blow. Serge held the elegant handkerchief to her nose and she blew.

"And worst of all"—Sarah gulped—"is that all of this is nothing compared to Kennedy's being shot."

"Oohyaiyai!" Serge smacked his forehead with the heel of his hand. "Yes, this day is terrible."

"And I feel ashamed now."

"Saar-ah! Vat are you talking about?" Vronsky paused. He looked genuinely perplexed. "Ashamed of vat?"

"I don't know. Everyone thinks that running away is the easy way out. They'll think I'm a coward. But there's nothing easy about it."

"But ashamed? Vy?"

"It's just that at one time I thought I might be running *to* something, and that would be great. I could imagine myself . . . oh—" She sobbed.

"Vat could you imagine yourself, Sarah?" Serge pressed.

"It sounds so dumb now."

"Vat?"

Sarah sniffed harder and rubbed her nose with the large square of linen. She swallowed. She must try to give the word dignity even if she herself did not deserve it. "I could imagine myself a pioneer." She gasped, then felt something inside her collapse.

"And?" Serge asked.

"And what?" An edge had crept into her voice.

"And now?"

"I'm nothing," Sarah whispered, her eyes bright with fear. "I'm just a fool in my own dreams."

"No, Saar-ah! I vill not let you talk this vay. It is true you vere running avay, but from nothing vorse than boredom and narrowness of human spirit. That is not so awful. I ran avay from the same thing myself many years ago."

Sarah looked up at Serge from the enormous hanky in which she had buried her face. "But that was political."

"So is your situation. Your school—it's just a smaller country, a different politics."

This was astounding to Sarah, but there was truth to it. Something stilled within her.

"Serge, I can't go back there. I love my mom and dad, but I can't go back to that school."

"I understand, but Saar-ah, first vee must try to reach your parents. I'm going to let Marla know that you're here, safe. And . . ." He paused. "You must not be upset vith Marla for . . . for entering this new vorld."

Well, that took the cake for euphemisms, Sarah thought. She looked at him suspiciously. "New world?"

"Okay, making love, having sex, losing one's virginity. I know vat you are feeling about your older sister. You feel very alone, left out. Ya, ya. I know."

"Did you have an older brother or sister?"

"No, no. But ven I lost my virginity I cried for myself, my old self, the vay you cry for your older sister and yourself!"

"She's going to be so angry with me for leaving her apartment like that."

"She might not be. Saar-ah, you are a very hard person to be angry vith."

They tried for two hours to get a call through to Indianapolis. Finally Vronsky sent a telegram:

*Sarah safe stop At Vronsky's in New York stop All is well*
*stop Will call when lines open stop Yours Serge stop*

Vronsky did not wake her when the first call came through. She slept until eight the next morning, when she heard a knock on her door. "Saar-ah." Vronsky peeked in. "It's your parents on the phone. Don't vorry, all is fine. Vee connected last night ven you vere fast asleep. Can you talk to them now?"

"Oh, Serge, I'm so nervous." She had slept in a dress shirt of his that came to her knees. He had given her an elaborate oriental-brocade caftan similar to the one he was wearing. Sarah's was so

211

enormous that she felt swallowed by it as she staggered toward the phone in Serge's library.

She picked up the receiver and shut her eyes tight, just as she had before she jumped off the twelve-foot diving board when she was ten years old.

"Hello," she whispered.

"Oh, baby!" sobbed her mother. "We've been so worried."

"Sarah!" Her dad was crying softly. "Thank God, my Sarah!"

For several seconds Sarah could hear only the most anguished hoarse sounds. It was then that she realized how terrible it had been for her parents. It suddenly dawned on her that her parents had probably imagined her mangled and bleeding on some highway, or kidnapped and murdered. She had done this to them. She had caused their worst and most paralyzing nightmare.

"Mom! Dad! I'm okay. Really, I'm fine."

"Sarah, we had no idea how alone . . ." Her mother's voice was laced with tremors and shallow breaths.

"It wasn't that, Mom." Sarah felt she had to shore her parents up in some way.

"Oh, Sarah, I know how frustrated you must have been. It's hard growing up. We forget." There were two shallow, raspy little breaths like gusts of wind striking gravel. "But Sarah, did you really have to run away?"

"I'm not sure exactly why I did it, Mom, but now that I've done it——" It was difficult to explain, but she had to try. "Now I have to stay awhile and think about it. This might sound weird, but I have some decisions to make." It did sound strange to Sarah, but she knew it was the truth.

"Ye-es . . ." Her mother sounded thoughtful, confused. "We certainly want you to have time to think. But there's plenty of time for decisions. Sarah, you have your whole life. . . . "

Decisions, Sarah knew her mother was suggesting, were to be made in adulthood. But some couldn't be postponed. Some had to be made now. Sarah felt once more the beats of her own heart. "But I can't be a shepherd anymore. You understand that, don't you?"

"Yes, darling. Do you want us to fly out today? Daddy has reservations on a late-afternoon flight."

"Look," said Sarah. This was even harder than she had feared. She knew she had hurt her parents terribly, caused them incredible anguish. She wanted them to know that she was okay. She wanted to hug and kiss them, but not right now. In this terrible week everyone needed someone to be near and to touch, but she could not see them just yet. "Mom. Dad." She spoke softly. "Could you wait just a couple of days?" She knew she would be stronger in a couple of days, calmer, better able to think.

"But Sarah . . ." Their voices were hesitant. "If you really feel this way . . . of course."

"I guess— Yes. I really do feel that it would be best." If her parents walked through that door right then, she knew that she would dissolve in a puddle of tears. They would fold her up in their arms and scold her for running away, and she would instantly become a baby. But babies didn't make decisions. She had already made one decision—not to be a shepherd. Her second had been to give herself time to think. "Mom, Dad, I took off without really thinking. But now I'm here and I've got to figure out why I did it, why this happened. I guess I was real desperate. I'm not desperate now. So maybe I can think better. I'm sorry. I'm sorry for scaring you."

"Oh, we were so scared, Sarah," her father said.

Vronsky, Sarah, Fong the houseman, and Bennett the cook,

like every household across America, were plastered to the television set, watching the grim aftermath of the tragedy: the tributes from around the world, the stunned faces of the cabinet secretaries as they disembarked from the plane that had been half a world away when the news came, the flare of klieg lights in the night and the silhouettes of the marine honor guard bearing the body to the White House and on to the rotunda, where it would lie in state until the funeral. They watched it all. Every meal was served in the library because that was where the television was.

On the second day Serge convinced Sarah to call Marla. She came immediately. Although it was awkward at first, Marla seemed to know and understand exactly what had troubled Sarah. She didn't mention Pinchas. She talked Sarah into going to the Metropolitan Museum of Art after lunch.

They were standing in a gallery filled with paintings. In spite of the bright, sun-splashed colors surrounding them, Sarah felt exceedingly dull, almost gray. She sensed that Marla, too, felt immune to the vibrancy of the painters' worlds.

Suddenly Marla turned to Sarah. "Oh, Sarah, I am so sorry!"

"What for?" Sarah said.

Marla's eyes were brimming with tears. "Because I cannot be, I haven't ever been, what you always wanted me to be."

Sarah was perplexed. "A virgin?"

"No." Marla laughed. "A perfect big sister."

"But you are so good, Marla. You're the best."

Sarah stopped. Her eyes began to fill. It was as if the two sisters were looking at each other through veils of falling rain. "Marla, can you believe what I did to Mom and Dad? They must have imagined me splattered dead on some highway. I can't believe that I've hurt them so, and I can't unhurt them now. Going back won't fix it. It's one thing not being the child of their dreams, but it's awful being the star of their worst *nightmare.*"

"Sarah! Sarah!" Marla paused. "Don't talk about dreams or nightmares. The important point is that neither you nor I are babies anymore."

A thrill ran through Sarah. They moved on, and the air seemed to tremble and brighten with the colors of the paintings.

It was on Tuesday, the day after the funeral, that Serge announced he was in dire need of some blinis. At twelve-thirty he and Sarah entered the Russian Tea Room, a restaurant on West Fifty-seventh Street. Heads turned as the famous dancer was ushered to his customary table in one of the upholstered booths. Waiters scurried. The maitre d' darted back and forth. A wine steward arrived with a bottle of champagne.

"Only one glass," Serge said.

"None for the young lady?"

Gosh, had she aged that much? "No, I'm just sixteen. Do you have a Coke?"

They ordered blinis with sturgeon, smoked salmon and caviar, and a *kulibiak*, which Serge promised Sarah she would love. She knew she would hate it, but food was so important to Vronsky and he hated to eat alone. He insisted that people share and rejoice and be as ecstatic over food as he was. It had something to do with the siege of Stalingrad back in World War II and having to eat unmentionable tiny furry mammals, Hattie had said.

The *kulibiak* was not as bad as Sarah had anticipated. Basically it was fish wrapped in thin pancakes and baked in a pastry crust. She had no quarrels with the dessert choice, a chocolate Malakoff.

"Heart-attack express!" Sarah said, digging into the rich custard-and-ladyfinger dessert.

"That's not vat Hattie vould call it!" Serge's eyes twinkled.

It was just at that moment that Sarah looked toward the door. "Oh-oh!" she gasped. "She might tell you in person!"

"Vat do you mean?" Serge looked startled.

"I mean, guess who's here?"

"Ah! Madame *Sil*verman!" gushed the maitre d'.

She was wearing a black armband tied around the sleeve of her bombardier jacket. Her eye was red. "I couldn't stay away, dear heart. I just couldn't." She hugged Sarah so tight that Sarah thought her ribs would crack.

The waiter had poured her a glass of champagne. "I was so good at counseling Shirley and Alf, telling them to keep calm, stay put for a few days, but here I am!"

"It's okay, Aunt Hattie." Sarah swallowed. "You probably understand better than they do why I had to get out of there."

"I think they understand now."

"Are they going to make me go back to Stuart Hall?"

"What would be the sense in that?" Hattie might see the sense, or lack of sense, in it, but Sarah wasn't sure her parents could. "I hope you notice, Serge, that I have not mentioned the twenty thousand calories on your plate."

"You are truly a peacemaker, Haa-tee!"

"Can you put me up along with Sarah? The painters won't be done in my apartment until November twenty-eighth."

"Of course."

After leaving the Russian Tea Room, Serge returned to his apartment. Hattie had declared she wanted to take a walk. She and Sarah strolled for several blocks. As they walked, they talked— about shepherds and ruined dreams. Sarah told Hattie about the newsboy and that long silent minute they shared at the stoplight. "I can't go back, Aunt Hattie. I don't know what I'm going to do. I've screeched to a halt, it seems. I'm not like one of your artists; you can't book my way through life."

"True." Aunt Hattie chuckled softly.

"I'm not bookable."

"That's more exciting."

"That's a big admission for a concert-talent manager to make."

"No it's not." She gave Sarah's arm a squeeze. "Besides, you're not unbookable. Look at that." She pointed to a poster in a window. A young girl with a farm-fresh face held a thin black infant in her arms. Above the photograph were the words THE PEACEFUL REVO-LUTION. It was a recruiting poster for the Peace Corps. "You see," Hattie said, "it takes something more than the ability to play Tchai-kovsky to do that."

Sarah was not sure why Hattie had said that. They walked a few more steps and stopped in front of a store window that had eight television sets all showing the same replays of Kennedy's fu-neral. On eight screens were identical images of the riderless horse prancing nervously in the dazzling sunlight and carrying the reversed boots in the stirrups. Hattie and Sarah held hands and watched the screens in silence. Suddenly it was as if the boots in the stirrups were turning around. And Sarah knew that things had not screeched to a halt. They would indeed proceed with great vigor, but at a slightly more measured pace, for there were still many things to be done.

Sarah's meeting with her parents was strange. Although only five days had passed, it could have been five years. They had kissed and hugged warmly, but now as her parents sat down the day before Thanksgiving in Serge's study they were oddly formal with her and she with them. They fumbled for words and talked around feelings for the first ten minutes. Fong had set out a tea service with cookies and minuscule cakes. There were a million little things to do with the tea—pouring the amber-colored liquid into shell-thin cups, adding clear hot water to dilute it from a second pot, squeezing lemon wedges with a small instrument designed specifically for that purpose, picking up small cubes of sugar with delicate tongs barely bigger than tweezers. Loud clatters and smallish talk punctuated the quiet. Finally Sarah set down a trembling cup and saucer.

Her parents were sitting on a small upholstered bench. On the wall was a charcoal sketch of a heroic-looking head from classical times. The temptation was to speak just past her dad's left ear to the drawing, to speak of inconsequential things. Behind her own head was another drawing, of a crumbling Roman ruin. Sarah had the feeling that her parents probably had a parallel temptation to address the once-glorious structure. There was no sense in being light-hearted or off-the-cuff. She could not erase the pain she had caused—there would always be this little scar in them and in her. But now it was time to speak.

"I know I made you scared. Real scared. I love you." Sarah paused. "But I can't go back."

"Yes. Hattie told us." Her father spoke. "You want to stay here with Hattie to finish high school."

"There are other high schools in Indianapolis," her mother said.

"I know." Sarah's breath caught short. "But I made this long trip here and even though I started it kind of without thinking—" She didn't finish. She noticed an odd and distant look in her dad's eyes. "What is it, Dad?"

"I was just remembering a short, long trip I once made." He paused. "My first jump as a paratrooper in 'forty-five."

Shirley's eyes rested on her husband. A fragile calm descended on the family.

"Maybe we should give it a try," Shirley whispered.

"You mean it, Mom?"

218

"Do you really think you and Hattie can live together?"

"Yes! I know it!"

"Well, Sarah," Alf said gently. "I guess you've learned the lesson in nuclear family physics."

Sarah's eyes brightened. It had been almost two years to the day since that atomic explosion and her vision of the fur-hatted particle blasting out of the nucleus.

# Significant Dates
# in the Chronology of
# Sarah Eloise Benjamin

February 16, 1964: Sarah celebrated her seventeenth birthday at the Russian Tea Room. Guests included her mother and father; Lieba, Shlomo, and Liberty Yossel Bell Rabinowitz; as well as Marla, Pinky, Serge, Hattie, Fong, Bennett; three new friends from her school in New York; an obscure Indian musician; and a surprise guest—Elaine Bauer, flown in courtesy of Alf and Shirley.

June 18, 1964: Sarah completed her junior year—four $A$'s and a $C^+$ in physics.

June 15, 1965: Sarah graduated from high school.

June 16, 1965: Sarah received notice of her acceptance into the Peace Corps. That same day she wrote to Cornell University and asked for a deferment of her admission until Peace Corps service was completed.

July 30, 1965: Sarah began her Peace Corps training in Westford, Massachusetts.

September 8, 1965: Sarah boarded an airplane at Kennedy International Airport bound for Sierra Leone via Dakar.

On November 4, 1965, the week pageant rehearsals usually began at Stuart Hall, Sarah wrote this letter to her parents:

Dear Folks,

My stomach is better. Quit worrying already—or as my favorite little kid, Moy, says: "Ees O.K., ees O.K. Eat Krispies no milk. Fix all." He's so great. Five going on sixty-five. I must admit that I do love it when they're short of help in the nursery. They have this screened porch right off the nursery and these two guys, other volunteers, built porch swings. And let me tell you, it is one of life's finest experiences to sit on a porch swing holding a little baby, whispering to it and crooning a tune through a Sierra night. Funny, most of the tunes I remember are those old Christmas pageant songs. I've got one little baby, Tumi, who just loves "Shepherds, Shake Off Your Drowsy Sleep."

I guess I have definitely shaken off the imposed drowsy sleep. I am very happy here. I think it's because I am part of a real pageant now and not a staged one. It feels so good.

Love, Sarah

P.S. Aunt Hattie wrote me that she's trying to get an African booking for Vronsky so she can come visit me. She wants me to find out where the nearest opera house is!!!